NURS

35p

Q1cc

Forced by injury to take a break from
nursing, Thea Westering counts herself
lucky to land a secretarial job on St
Stephen's orthopaedic ward. And even
luckier to work with attractive registrar
James Mayling . . .

NURSE IN WAITING

BY

JANET FERGUSON

MILLS & BOON LIMITED
15–16 BROOK'S MEWS
LONDON W1A 1DR

First published in Great Britain 1984 by Robert Hale Limited

This edition published 1985 by Mills & Boon Limited

© Janet Ferguson 1984

Australian copyright 1985 Philippine copyright 1985

ISBN 0 263 74966 5

Set in 10 on 12 pt Linotron Times
03–0285–52,000

Photoset by Rowland Phototypesetting Ltd Bury St Edmunds, Suffolk Made and printed in Great Britain by Richard Clay (The Chaucer Press) Ltd Bungay, Suffolk

CHAPTER ONE

'YOU LOOK ghastly, Thea!'

I knew I did, I didn't need Wendy to tell me, at least not in quite such unremitting tones.

'You might just as well,' she went on, staring up at me from the platform, 'have let me drive you. Why put yourself through these hoops?'

'I shall be perfectly all right,' I said, as the train began to judder, getting itself all ready to move out. Wendy was seeing me off at Victoria, I was going down to Sussex, it was early May, it was Sunday afternoon.

It had been a Sunday afternoon exactly three months ago when I had been involved in a rail disaster just outside London Bridge. This was my first train journey since then. And I was nervous, I was shaking all over, I was virtually a jelly. It was all I could do to stop myself joining Wendy on the platform, and making for the nearest telephone to ring Uncle John. For what was I doing, what was I thinking of, taking a clerical job? I was a nurse, an orthopaedic-trained nurse, with certificates to prove it. The trouble was I had also got a knee without a knee-cap. It had been fractured in the accident, and had had to be removed. This had put me in hospital for eight weeks, followed by a month at home—at home in the flat which Wendy and I shared. We were both nurses at St Mildred's Hospital in South-East London. We had trained together and been friends ever since.

It had felt weird being a patient in the hospital where I

worked, especially in the ward where I worked—namely Female Orthopaedic. I had been an impatient patient too, wanting to do things too soon, but in no way could the process be hurried up. Professor Whelan had been very definite as he'd flexed and rotated my knee: 'Now you know as well as I do, Nurse Westering, that repaired tendons can rupture if they're too soon exposed to excess strain. You can do a sedentary job, if you like, but you can't go back to nursing, not for another three or four months at least.'

He was right, and I knew he was, which is why I'd been sensible and decided to accept Uncle John's offer of a job at Lowhampton-on-Sea. The job was that of Ward Secretary in his Orthopaedic Unit. I would also be asked to type for his Registrar.

Uncle John (my father's brother) is a surgeon of repute. He has his own Unit in St Stephen's Hospital, on the fourth floor of the Tower Block. He had made the job, over the telephone to me, sound very attractive indeed: 'You'll have your own office, Thea . . . no one to pressure you. The usual secretary, Mrs Frewin, is having an operation. The time period fits exactly, it could have been made for you. You'll live with us at The Moorings, of course; that goes without saying. Your Aunt Meg's already spring-cleaning your room.'

So I had said 'yes' without too much thought. I was tired of being idle. I had gone ahead and made the arrangements which had brought me to this moment . . . standing like a jelly in the train. It jolted and jangled, and began to ease forward; Wendy grimaced and waved. I waved back, and sat down, watching the platforms slide by. I sat with clenched hands and a knotted inside as the train drummed over the river. I fought down rising panic with all my might.

After Croydon I began to feel better, but couldn't settle to read, so I closed my eyes and let my thoughts roll back over the weeks—not right back to the accident, I'm no masochist, but back to my sojourn in hospital, to the following month at the flat, grinding along to Physio on a stick. After a time the stick was discarded and I didn't so much as limp. It was then that my hopes had risen high, had foamed right over the top. Surely they would let me go back to nursing, surely my knee was all right. But they didn't, there was no question of it, not for another four months, and then had come the offer from Uncle John.

Wendy had been all against my acceptance, she hadn't minced her words: 'Honestly, Thea, it's a crazy idea. The Staff will resent you like mad. They'll all know you're the Chief's niece, they'll think you've been planted there. You'll be viewed askance, like the spectre at the feast!'

'Then I'll have to ride it out, won't I?' I had felt a little annoyed, 'After all, it's only for four months.'

I wondered what James Mayling, the Registrar, would be like. Uncle John had called him a sterling character, which probably meant he was awkward, and unbending, one of the stoic sort. I knew I would work in an office attached to Lytton Ward, which was Male Orthopaedic, I would cope with its myriad forms. I also knew that Mr Mayling and Sister were engaged, which added an interesting fillip to it all.

Uncle John's secretary, Miss Reenham, was attached to Vinton Ward—Lytton Ward's female counterpart. The width of a landing divided the wards, so we might not meet very much: 'But she'll help you, Thea,' Uncle had said, 'she's a mite temperamental, you know, but very efficient. You can go to her if you're stuck.'

I was likely to be stuck, I was quite sure, for although I knew ward procedure, and a little about its clerical work, and a lot about orthopaedics, the shorthand and typing course I had taken had been in my last year at school, before I had started my nurses' training, which was five years ago. I had practised my speeds from time to time, but on the whole I was slow. When I told Uncle John this, all he had said was pooh.

He always poohs and puffs away what he doesn't want to hear. He's short and square, and sandy-haired, and excessively good-hearted. He and Aunt Meg live in a house called The Moorings in Pleydon village. Pleydon is three miles out of Lowhampton town. My parents live on the island of Ibiza, both of them are writers. I could, of course, have gone home to them for the following three or four months, but apart from the journey which is over-long, it wouldn't have been very fair. They had come to London after the accident and stayed in South-wark a month. I knew enough about their routine to appreciate what that had meant. In no way could I disrupt it again, at any rate not quite so soon. It wouldn't do. Writers need to be quiet.

Aunt Meg was meeting me at Lowhampton Station. I roused and looked at my watch. It was four-thirty, half the journey was done. Soon after this the train began to pour itself through the South Downs. The gloomy tunnel into which it plunged turned the windows to looking-glass. In them I could see my reflection, my black centre-parted hair, long-lidded eyes, wide mouth, the outline of my sweater, the gold chain knotted at my throat. I fiddled with the chain, twisted it round, my thoughts raced backwards again. What a long, long time it was since I'd been in uniform. What would I wear as a Ward Secretary—a white coat, I supposed. I sighed a little as the train burst out into the sunlight again. My reflection paled to a shadowy shape, and I reached for my denim jacket as a stiff little salty breeze blew round my ears.

At Mear Park, the last-but-one stop before Low-hampton, a man and two little boys got on. They sat in the double seat opposite me. They appeared to have been on a ramble. They all three, the man included, wore stout walking shoes. They were breathing hard, as though they'd had to run. The man was attractive, compellingly so, I couldn't help staring at him. He was tall and long-legged, his hair was tawny, the thick kind that likes to rise up. His eyes were grey, or I thought they were, they met mine head on, as he stretched his waist to unzip his anorak. Hastily, and in some confusion, I transferred my gaze to the boys. They were twins around six or seven years old, the smaller one wore glasses, a bunch of primroses wilted in his hands. The other boy looked at the blooms, as one or two dropped on the floor:

'You shouldn't have picked them, they'll only die.'

'Daddie said I could, and they won't die.'

'They will!'

'They won't! Don't touch them! Leave them alone!'

Their voices were piping, disturbingly shrill, their father urged quietness, then turned his face to the window and stared out. He had a long stubborn jaw, I noticed, and a gripped look to his mouth. He looked like a man beset with problems, but alas, we all have those. He moved and I quickly averted my eyes as he looked at the boys again. They were bickering, they were probably over-tired.

'You should never pick wild flowers, William,' the bigger child said smugly. His hair was tawny like his father's, he had the same dogged look.

'They're for Nan!' The little one's glasses were too big for his face, he wrinkled his nose to try to get them straight. 'They're for Nan,' he repeated, hugging the flowers squashily to his chest.

'She won't want *those!*'

'Yes, she will.'

'She won't!'

'She will . . . she WILL!'

Their voices reached shouting pitch, making passengers turn their heads, and click with their tongues, and mutter amongst themselves. The man slewed round in his seat, he told the children off. He did so very quietly, but very soundly too. Sitting so close I could hear every scolding word: 'If you two boys don't behave yourselves, then it's bed when we get home. Now, sit up straight, keep your feet off the seats, and try to talk quietly.' They subsided, abashed. I felt rather sorry for them.

My sympathy was misplaced, however, for less than five minutes later, the bigger boy began to elbow the little one in the ribs. When this produced no quick result, he snatched at his bunch of flowers, jerked at the heads, and they scattered all over the floor. The commotion then was ear-splitting; the boys began to fight, to scuffle and roll between the seats, between the man's legs and mine. Nervous of my knee, terrified of kicks, I swung my legs to the side, but even so I couldn't avoid one flying, stoutly-shod foot, which landed with a thump against my shin.

I gasped, cried out, leapt to my feet, caught at the overhead rack. The blow had in no way touched my knee, had been nowhere near my scar, but I tended to guard the whole of that leg virtually with my life, for remembered pain makes for cautiousness. It makes for a snap-flash temper too, when danger zooms in close, or has just passed, leaving an aftermath. It was the aftermath that was on me now, precipitating anger, all of it directed at the man: 'For goodness' sake,' I stepped over the boys who still rolled about on the floor, 'for goodness' sake, can't you control them! They're little better than hooligans! They've no business to be in a train at all!'

He glared at me, his jaw went tight, he looked down at his sons. Jerking them up from the filthy floor, he sat one on each side of him. His face was as darkly suffused as theirs, mine was clammy and pale. I *felt* the paleness, the pricking of sweat on my lip. I sat down, I couldn't stand: people were turning round. The carriage was the sort with a centre corridor, which facilitated staring, comments flowed . . . comments which made things worse: 'Children these days' . . . 'No proper control' . . . 'I blame the parents, you know' . . . 'I don't care what you say, it starts in the home.'

I felt sick and ill, and ashamed too. How *could* I have shouted like that. 'I hope you're not hurt,' the man said, but I glimpsed the disdain in his eyes. No parent likes his child criticised. He made the boys apologise, which they did like chanting parrots. Then silence reigned, there was just the gush of the train.

I so much wanted to take back my words, to explain my over-reaction, but the man's expression, his whole demeanour, put me off completely, kept me as rigidly silent as the boys. In any case, there was no time left, we were nearly into Lowhampton. Here was the red-brick signal box, the pull and curve of the line, the ends of the platforms, the struts of the station roof.

The man and the boys got out on the instant the train stopped moving. The sight of their empty seat was a small rebuff. I got up and a youth in a track-suit helped me out with my cases, found a help-yourself trolley, and loaded them on for me. I wheeled the trolley along to the barrier, still feeling rather uptight. But how silly and childish to mind so much that an unknown man thought me shrewish . . . for he *had* thought that, I had seen it in his eyes.

There was no sign of him or the boys, when I came out from the station and stood in the yard, looking for Aunt Meg. A white Lancia began to move forward, and I saw her at the wheel. She was smiling at me, and lifting a hand, her pepper-and-salt hair scuffed by the sun-glasses thrust on top of her head. She was with me in seconds, hugging me close, smelling of Lifebuoy soap, and face powder, and faintly of the sea: 'Thea, darling . . . what marvellous luck . . . to have you for four whole months!' She swung my cases into the boot as though they were featherweights. She clicked it shut, and gave it a bottomly slap.

Aunt Meg is tall and big-boned, a little mannish, perhaps, but her face, though plain, is a good one to look at, and her eyes are beautiful, a warm brown, narrow, and twinkly, and kind.

'It was good of Uncle John to get me the job on

the Unit.' We began to cruise slowly down Queen's Road.

'He thought it was just the thing for you, and we so much wanted you here,' Aunt Meg took a left hand turning to cut off the worst of the traffic: Lowhampton is a busy seaside town. 'You can have my old Morris,' she said, 'to run around in down here. It'll save the fag of buses. I expect you can drive with your knee.'

'Oh, heavens, yes,' I said. 'It's practically all right. I'm sure I could have gone back to nursing, but in no way would they let me. You know what orthopaedic surgeons are.'

'Living with one, I ought to!' Aunt Meg laughed. I joined in, it was only too easy; her laughter was infectious. She was like a tonic, my spirits began to rise.

We turned on to the coast road and joined the traffic stream. The sea was on our right-hand side, a mixture of blue and indigo; there were bulky clouds, a heavy cumulus. 'John would have come to the station with me,' she slipped her sun-glasses down, 'but he was called out to the hospital to an accident case, after lunch. James Mayling was off duty, so of course John had to go. He'll be somewhere in that gaggle of buildings,' she jerked her chin at the hospital, which sprawled on our left, dwarfing the big hotels. I screwed downwards in my seat to view the tower block. There it stood, twelve levels high, like a giant upended matchbox, inelegant, but functional to a degree. I had seen it before, many times, but had never thought to work there, at any rate not as other than a nurse.

And perhaps my aunt guessed what was passing through my head, for her next remark was a follow-on from my thoughts: 'It'll be a complete change for you, won't it, having an office job?'

'Yes, you can say that again.' We were passing a Southdown bus; its pale green sides filled my window, I stared at the road in front.

'So, how do you think you'll make out?'

'Pretty amazing,' I said. And once again we laughed together, as we left the traffic behind, and approached Pleydon village which lay in a fold in the Downs.

As soon as we got to The Moorings, even before I'd had time to sit down, Aunt Meg dragged me through to the sitting-room to show me her latest find. She collected antiques, mostly china and glass, and some of it was valuable. Her hobbies were legion and she said she loved to indulge. The shallow dish which she passed me was delicate and unusual; it was blue and white, with a narrow fluted rim. 'I like it, *very* much,' I turned it round in my hand.

'Hugh got it for me,' she said, in the careful kind of voice she always used when speaking to me of Hugh.

'He's been home again, has he?' I replaced the dish in the cabinet, closed the glass door and turned the key. Hugh Delter was Aunt Meg's nephew (her sister Alison's son) and five years ago I had fallen in love with him. We had been at The Moorings on holiday, I had been seventeen, Hugh twenty-five; I had thought him fabulous. His job added to his glamour; he was employed by Elverstein's, the auctioneers and art dealers, with sale-rooms all over the world. He had been on the brink of going to New York for a term of several years: 'But I'll be home often,' he'd said, 'several times a year. We can meet in London, have a great time. We must never, ever lose touch.' Yet even as he said this I had known the avowal meant little. There had been a far-away look in his eyes, a slackening of interest. Hugh had been looking forward to pastures new.

'He's home for good,' Aunt Meg was saying, and I swung round in surprise. Her back was to me, she was opening the patio doors. 'He's left Elverstein's.' She secured the doors, and came in dusting her hands.

'Left Elverstein's! *Has* he?' I had to admit to surprise. 'But why, Aunt Meg, and where is he working now?'

'In Lowhampton, would you believe!' She laughed at the look on my face. 'He's gone into partnership with Carl Geeson—you know, of Geesons' Antiques. There's a decent flat over the shop, he's moved in there. I gave him a few bits of furniture out of our loft.'

'I never thought he'd leave Elverstein's. He used to boast about it.'

'Things change, Thea, people change; perhaps Hugh himself has changed. He's been keen to have a share in a business for some time now. It wasn't a sudden decision at all. There was much to be arranged.'

Yes, I thought, like money to buy the partnership with. I guessed this had most likely come from Aunt Meg. She adored Hugh, she always had, and who could possibly blame her? His mother was divorced and lived in Bath with a man he didn't like. And as well as being Hugh's aunt, Aunt Meg was his godmother. She was mine too, which made a link of sorts.

'So he's putting down roots in Lowhampton, is he?' I strained to sound natural. The trouble is one can never forget one's very first romance. Little drifty memories and touches come teasingly back.

'Nothing could please me more,' she said. She

perched on the arm of a chair, straining the skirt of her bolster-type dress to highly dangerous limits. I stared at it, tight as a drum across her knees. 'You won't mind him coming here, will you?'

'I can hardly wait,' I said. 'I'm just surprised that you didn't mention any of this on the phone.'

'John thought it might put you off, that you might decide not to come.'

'Good grief!' My laugh rang out, 'I'm twenty-two years old. You can't think I've spent the last five years hankering after Hugh, missing out on exciting dates, missing out on fun. I work in a hospital, males abound, I've been enjoying myself. Oh, I don't say I've ever gone in very deep, but I've had my little flutters. Falling in love with Hugh was like cutting a first tooth—painful, perhaps, but scarcely crippling for life.'

'Sorry, dear.'

'So you should be,' I said, as I crossed the room. I took a framed snapshot off a bookcase and studied it close to. It showed Hugh and me in the garden of The Moorings, dressed in tennis clothes. We were posed against the bottom fence, the one on the cliff edge. Behind our heads—both of them dark—was the blue of the sea and sky, the line of horizon, straight and razor sharp. That had been the day Hugh had said my eyes were mysterious: 'And one day, Theadora Westering, you're going to be beautiful, like a Spanish dancer, tall, and lissom, and dark.' Hugh had never been lost for words, but his silver-tongued prophecy had been wide of the mark, as the following years were to prove. In no way am I beautiful—striking, yes, perhaps; for with black hair, and being thin, I can go in for trendy clothes and brilliant colours, and get away with both. At seventeen I had been all legs, and my clothes had been disastrous, I had lacked the art of making the best of myself. I had lacked the art of subtlety too, all my innermost feelings had been on show, had ballooned out over my head. No wonder Hugh's interest had waned. What had there been to hold it? He had been my first boy-friend, a long, long time ago. 'I suppose,' I said, peering at our two pictured faces, 'that he's just as fabulous looking.'

'Even more so, I think.' She came to look over my shoulder, 'He's grown a moustache, you know. It sets him off. I'm surprised he's not married.'

'Is he so irresistible, then?'

'Don't be silly, dear.' She took the photograph, and set it back in place. 'He's away just now,' she added, 'at a sale in Exeter. He won't be back for two weeks. He knows you're here, of course. He was horrified when we told him you had been in that accident. He said to tell you how very sorry he was.'

'Nice of him to be concerned.' I went upstairs to change. But peeling off jeans and sweater in the guest-room that faced the sea, I had to admit that it might be interesting to meet Hugh again. He might ask me out; it would liven things up—not that life down here was dull. There was plenty to do in Lowhampton, especially in the summer, but one needed someone to be able to do it *with*.

When I went back downstairs in my green smock dress and boots, I found Uncle John there, full of exuberance: 'Well, how was your journey, how was your journey?' (he always repeated his words). He pressed me into a chair and patted my head.

'I was on tenterhooks at first,' I admitted, 'but

improved as time went on.' I forebore to mention the incident in the train.

'Marvellous girl, marvellous girl! A true Westering!' His smile burst out, buckling his cheeks, showing his gold-lined tooth. He went to mix me what he called his 'special aperitif', crashing the ice about like castanets.

I wasn't surprised when, with supper over, he wanted to examine my knee, for it's a very incurious surgeon who can resist the opportunity of having a good look at a colleague's work. 'It's good,' he said, when he'd finished rotating, 'very good indeed, but I know how painful it must have been at the time it happened, Thea.'

'It was horrific, awful . . . and I don't mean my knee, but the whole disaster,' I said. And just for a second I was back in that accident, back in that tangled space. I could hear the falling, the creaking, the tearing, the bang of exploding glass, the reek of burning, the wailing of a child. 'There were people hurt all round me,' I said, 'and I was powerless to help. I couldn't move, I was jammed tight, flattened under debris. There was so much going on all around me, and I couldn't move an inch. Oh, if only I could have freed myself, crawled out and done something for *someone*!'

'Like saving a life—a nurse's dream. My dear little Dora!' Sometimes Uncle John called me that when he felt emotional. 'It's a wonder you didn't lose your own.'

Later, on the patio, with the setting sun flaming our faces, he told me about the accident case he'd admitted that afternoon. 'Spinal injury, young chap of twenty, damage to the neural arch. I shall have to operate, fix in a plate to protect the spinal cord. You'll have all the forms to prepare on the ward tomorrow, Thea. I've got to be at Wellbridge by ten, got a hip replacement there, but I hope to get up to Lytton Ward early on, to see the boy. You know you start at half-eight, don't you? You can make your own debut?'

'I'm used to debuts,' I told him, but underneath the table, I crossed my fingers. I hoped I'd make the grade.

As it happened, my entrance, or debut, went off very well. Sister Filey met me at the lifts, and introduced me all round, made sure that I knew the layout of the place. She was very different from what I'd expected. She was small, curvacious, fair-haired. Her nose and cheekbones were dusted with freckles, she had spiky-lashed hazel eyes. She looked like the sort of woman who ought to have married young and had a large family. I knew she was thirty-plus. She was engaged to James Mayling, I remembered, so there'd still be time for that family. Plenty of women had babies in their thirties; it was almost the fashion these days, and Sister Ruth Filey looked nowhere near her age.

She took me over to Vinton Ward to meet Uncle's secretary, Miss Reenham, whom I found to be austere. She was grey-haired, with piercing blue eyes, and a handshake like a vice. She was vice-like altogether really, I eased the cramps from my fingers, I promised to join her for lunch at one p.m. in the Staff Canteen. 'Then after today,' she added, rather spoiling the invitation, 'I'm sure you'll be able to manage on your own.'

Back on Lytton I inspected the ward office—my domain for the next four months. It was on the opposite side of the corridor from Sister's, just outside the ward doors. One of its windows looked into the ward, the other out on to the street. The street one showed the sea and rooftops, the rows of little houses, the Eye Hospital on the other side of the road.

Mrs Frewin's white coat, which I found on the door, fitted me fairly well girthwise, but was too short and looked ridiculous. 'I should take it off,' Sister said. 'Send down to Stores for another.' She had entered my room on silent feet, she was quietly-spoken too. She looked at my cream silk blouse and brown skirt (the most sombre things in my wardrobe) and said how she envied me being tall and slim.

'I suppose we all want to be different from the way Nature made us,' I said, hanging the white coat back on the door. I turned to the desk, took the cover off the typewriter, and heaved a sigh of relief. It was the same make as the one I used for letters in the flat. I had been afraid I might be faced with a complicated computer one, with a memory bank and words coming up on a screen.

'Your first task,' Sister was saying in her low, almost whispering voice, 'is to get out the case-notes ready for the round. Sir John will be up early to see the spinal patient. Mr Mayling will see the latest post-ops, I expect. Here's the list, and the notes are there,' she pointed to the cabinets which were ranged like steel bastions round the walls. 'You know where I am if you want me, don't you, exactly opposite.' She stood with her back against the jamb of the door.

'Yes, I do, and I'll be all right,' I glanced at the list in my hand, I was well used to getting case-notes out. I hoped she would leave me on my own, but she seemed inclined to linger. I could feel her staring as I pulled the steel drawers out.

'It's good of you to help us, especially in this capacity.'
She was just, very slightly, I thought, overdoing
the welcome. I assured her I was used to clerical
work:

'At St Mildred's,' I told her, 'we don't have ward
secretaries. The nursing staff have to cope, which I
suppose is useful experience that will stand me in good
stead!' I tried a smile, but hers in return was strained and
a little uneasy. She looked worried, as though she had
something on her mind.

'It's such a bonus too,' she said, 'that you're able to
write shorthand. James . . . Mr Mayling, is one of those
men who dislike putting work on a tape. I tell him he'll
have to come to it some time. Eileen Frewin spoils him,
but then most people do.' She went out, closing the
door.

She couldn't have known that mentioning shorthand
made me quake in my shoes. It was my weak spot, my
Achilles heel, I tried not to think about it. Instead I
applied myself to the notes and found them all without
trouble. I had put the last set in the truck (used for
wheeling them round the ward), when I heard the
approaching mumble of voices in the passage. My door
burst open and in came Uncle John:

'Thea, there you are, m'dear, all settled down, I see.
Now, James . . .' he made a beckoning sign to a looming
shape in the doorway. I tucked in my blouse and
straightened my skirt, unconsciously bracing myself, but
even so nothing prepared me for the jolting shock I got
when I saw who was coming into the room.

He was a tall and tawny man, with a long stubborn
jaw. His face had the kind of brown seamed look
that comes from the wind and the sea; his eyes were

grey and deep-set; his brows shot up when he saw
me . . .

James Mayling was my antagonist of the train . . .

CHAPTER TWO

'WE MET yesterday,' he said abruptly, as Uncle John introduced us.

'Met? But how?' Uncle looked flummoxed. 'You didn't mention it, Thea.'

'We didn't know one another's identity, not until this moment.' James Mayling's eyes turned to him. 'We met in the train,' he said. 'My car broke down at Gattley Hill, I had the twins with me. We ran all the way to Mear Park Station, just managed to catch the train. We happened to sit down opposite your niece.'

'And exchanged pleasantries? Well, how *nice*!' Uncle's bland look returned. 'You know, James, the arm of coincidence is remarkably long at times.'

'So it would seem, sir.'

My face burned, but Uncle carried on, giving him various details about my knee. 'You must have a look at it some time, James. I'm sure Thea won't mind. They've done a superb job on her, it's Whelan's work, you know . . . marvellous chap . . . no one to beat him for knees. He's done a mass of research, too, got his own lab at St Mildred's. I thought he was about to retire, but I may have got it wrong. Yes, yes, Sister, we're just coming.' Sister Filey was looking anxious, and a little impatient; she wanted to start the round. 'We haven't got a house-man at the moment, which makes it hard for James,' Uncle John whispered, as he squeezed past to the door.

My mind turned over like a tumble-drier, as I watched them go on to the ward. What an *incredible* thing to have happened, to have met James Mayling like that. It couldn't have happened . . . yet I knew it had, and the twins, the boys, were his sons. Was he divorced then, or a widower? I thought most likely the former, I felt his aura was that of a quarrelsome man. And why, oh why, had I been so remiss as not to ask more about him. I ought to have done so, have asked Uncle John, but somehow or other, last night, our conversation had been almost solely concerned with family matters. We had discussed Mother's latest book, which was called *The Loving Reprisal*. Sometimes I wondered where she got her titles from.

I began to type the bed-list, and in pairing up names and numbers, managed to push James Mayling out of my mind. I was getting on reasonably well, for bed-lists aren't difficult, when I heard Uncle John pass my door, heard his sung out 'Goodbye'. He was off to Wellbridge County Hospital to perform the hip operation. James Mayling and Sister were still engrossed in the ward. I looked through my viewing window and watched them moving along. His white coat hung loosely on him, it had a vent at the back. It was slightly crumpled where he'd sat down and hadn't bothered to smooth it. Most male doctors' coats have a wrinkle at the hem. Sister was moving neatly, adroitly, solemnly, in his wake. Her navy-blue dress fitting her snugly, the tight petersham belt emphasising the curves of hips and bust. I watched them move to the bedside of a patient on sliding traction. She drew the curtains, screening them from my sight. They were engaged, I remembered, engaged to be married. Well, the best of luck to them both. I felt that

Ruth Filey, despite her mild air and quiet, whispering voice, could, when the need arose, put her foot down good and hard. She would be patient with children, I was quite sure, but they'd have to behave themselves. She wouldn't stand for fighting in a train.

I had finished the bed-list, and was sorting a pile of reports marked 'filing', when the telephone rang in Sister's office, and feeling I ought to answer it, I got up and crossed the corridor. At the same moment she and James Mayling appeared at the ward doors. Sister called out, 'I'll answer it, thanks,' and went into her room. James Mayling followed me into mine.

I was nervous, but tried not to show it. My mouth was very dry. He closed the door and the click it gave was like a kind of knell. Was he going to mention that business in the train?

'I've some dictation for you, Miss Westering,' he said. He was pulling the truck of notes. 'I'd like to get two discharge reports done, and one or two letters to doctors. No doubt Sir John explained that part of Mrs Frewin's duties—temporarily yours—is to type any stuff I may have.'

'Yes, he told me.'

'Please sit down.'

I sat, and so did he, one of his knees jarred against the desk. I had laid a notebook and pencil ready, I reached out and drew them towards me, I opened the notebook and waited for him to start. I felt more and more tense by the second. What would it be like? Would he go too fast, would I have to stop him? But he wasn't ready yet, he bent to the truck of notes and jerked out a file. Slip . . . slip . . . slip . . . slip . . . I could hear him leafing the pages: 'I'm a little rushed today,' he said, and I promptly

wrote that down, then realised he was talking directly to
me.

'I see.'

'I'm due in Theatre at ten.'

'I see,' I said again. I stared at my notebook, at the
ruled faint lines, at the shadow my knuckles made.
Hurry up and start, get it over, and let me be able to do
it. Please, please, don't let him go too fast.

He began at last, I began to write, and at first it wasn't
too bad. His pace was moderate, his voice clear, I was
going to be all right. But then without warning he went
more quickly, he was getting into his stride. My brain
grappled with the difficult passages, my hand and fingers
dragged. But I still kept up . . . I still kept up . . . I might
just make it yet. The whole world filled with the sound of
his voice.

The letter was to a local doctor about a young boy
patient who had an abnormal angle between the neck
and shaft of his femur. It wasn't easy to transpose the
medical words into shorthand. He must have known it,
but he still went on and on. 'There is an external
rotational deformity . . .' he slowed up very slightly,
'and a coxa vara with a positive Trendelenberg sign.
X-ray shows the degree of displacement of the femoral
epiphysis.' He lifted his head, his tone altered. 'I expect
you can spell "epiphysis"?'

'I can, yes,' I scrawled the word in longhand for
absolute safety. 'I can also,' I said, disliking the smile
which played around his mouth, 'spell "Trendelenberg". I have come across it before.'

'I was forgetting you were a nurse.' He flipped the
case-notes over the desk. 'Tidy those, will you. They
seem to have got in a mess.'

I caught the notes against my chest, the paper spread out like a fan: 'I *am* a nurse,' I corrected, 'the terms are familiar to me. I'm a secretary only for the time being, until my knee's got strong.'

'Quite,' he said, with another small smile, which made me want to hit him, made me want to say something outrageously rude. He was opening yet another file, and before I could gather my wits, he was off again, dictating very fast: 'Re Norman Alexander,' he intoned, 'admitted 16th April' . . . faster and faster . . . faster and faster . . . I could only just keep up. He was doing it on purpose, I knew he was, I wouldn't let him beat me . . . faster and faster . . . his voice went on and on. He was standing, walking up and down. I could hear his shoes squeaking, and once when he passed me, his arm brushed against my chair. He got to the end of the letter at last, dictated several more just as quickly, then pushed the truck away.

I knew he was looking at me as I scrawled the last few words. I was hot all over, my fingers were slippery, my pencil was down to the wood. Oh please, I prayed, please don't let him ask me to read any back. I couldn't do it, I heard him flop down in his chair.

'Is everything all right, Miss Westering?' he asked quite kindly. The kindness surprised me, I assured him that it was. 'You don't want to verify anything?'

'No, thank you, it's all very clear.'

'In that case,' he pushed himself up, 'I'll see you at five o'clock. That's when I like to sign my letters, in time to catch the post. We may as well stick to Eileen Frewin's routine.'

'Yes, I agree.' My voice was stiff, almost as stiff as my body which felt a hundred, as I, too, got to my feet. You don't need to worry, I thought, as he snapped open the door, and made off down the passage on urgent feet. I shan't deviate by so much as a comma from Eileen Frewin's ways. It'll be all I can do to get your letters typed.

But perhaps if I could have been left alone to wrestle with them then, there would have been a chance of everything going well. Such an idyllic state of affairs wasn't to be, however. No sooner had James Mayling left my room than Sister entered it. She laid what looked like a roster on my machine. 'It's the Duty Roster for typing, please. I'd like a top and two carbons. The top copy goes to the SNO, and one of the carbons to me; the second carbon is pinned to the board in the Nurses' Duty Room. The same applies to the Work List . . . now, where have I put that?' She dived into her dress pocket and pulled out two more sheets: 'I wonder if you would mind doing these before you start doing anything else. They're usually put on the board on Sundays, we're one day behind. Oh, wait, though . . .' she clapped a hand worriedly to her head, 'perhaps first of all you could go down to X-ray. It's on Level 3, next to Theatres. I want Mr Charles Beckett's films, he's the fractured mandible.'

I smiled and nodded like a mandarin, I must have looked idiotic. I followed her out, then she stopped and turned, and I all but stepped on her feet. 'Sorry.' She looked up at me, I topped her by half a head, 'I suppose you couldn't, whilst off the Unit, take some specimens down to the labs. It would save me sending one of the nurses, we're understaffed this morning.'

'I don't think I know where the labs are.' We had turned into the sluice, where a row of little bottles and jars stood labelled in a rack.

'Here, put them in this,' she gave me a square dispensary basket. 'The labs are in the main building, separate from the tower. When you get to ground level you take the covered way to Physical Medicine, turn right by the Renal Unit, then straight down the colonnade. The labs are at the bottom, on the left of Haematology.'

As clear as daylight, I thought to myself, but all I said was, 'Thank you.' I packed the basket, and when I turned round Sister Filey had gone, silently back to her grossly understaffed ward.

By the time I had finished my errands, and typed the urgent lists, it was close on eleven o'clock, so now for the letters, I thought. But a further obstacle reared its head in the shape of a telephone call. This meant I would have to go to Physio to fetch a patient back: 'He's waiting now,' the voice at the other end said. The Physiotherapy Department was part of Uncle's Unit, but it was on the other side, at the back of Vinton Ward. As I walked there, traversing landings, diving down runways of corridors, I wondered how he could possibly think . . . could possibly imagine, that my job as a secretary would benefit my knee.

I found the patient waiting for me outside the plaster room. He was in a wheelchair, with his right leg extended on a board. He was a nice-looking man in his early fifties, his name was Martineau, Robert Martineau; he had had a broken leg.

'A compound fracture,' he told me, as we started the journey back. 'I manage Hartington's Bookshop, you know. Fell off the top of some steps. I was getting some books down off a shelf, must have been clumsy, I expect. Done in a minute, a second even, then all these weeks in here. I had a wound infection too, which delayed things even more. Still, it's good to be out of plaster. Now it's physio every day. Not that I mind the exercises, but they take it out of you.'

'Yes, I know they do,' I said with feeling, and I smiled at the back of his head, which was all I could see as I pushed the chair along. He had a good thick head of black hair, threaded through with grey. He asked if I knew how Eileen Frewin was.

'To be honest, I don't,' I told him, 'I only started today, but I'm sure if you asked Sister she would make enquiries for you.'

'I'll find out somehow,' he said, as I turned his chair back to front. I butted the doors to the ward corridor inwards with my rear, wedged the left-hand door with my foot, pulled the chair swiftly through. The doors swung to with a soft thud as we went down the corridor, face forwards again, I heard Mr Martineau laugh.

'That's a neat manoeuvre, and not the first time you'd done it, I'll be bound!'

'I've done it more times than I can count, but not here,' I smiled. I told him how I came to be at St Stephen's Hospital, I also told him a little about my knee.

'So, you know what it's like to be laid up.'

'I certainly do,' I replied.

'But it's fortunate that you could come here, I mean, for Eileen's sake. I know she'll be glad that her job's in good hands. She's very conscientious. Sometimes I think she puts work before everything else.'

A nurse came forward at that point and wheeled him to his bed. He obviously knew Mrs Frewin well. Had romance blossomed there, I wondered? Had they known each other before he came in here? As I turned into the office there was Sister again, standing at my desk, with another list in her hand: 'Mrs Frewin,' she said, 'often helps with lunches, sees them given out . . . supervises, in other words; she checks them off on this,' she handed the clipboarded list to me: 'These are special diets. We don't have many of those, praise be, just three diabetics, one non-fat, one high-fibre, and one low-residue. The fractured jaw, Mr Beckett, is on liquids only, of course. His jaws are wired, but he manages a straw. Oh yes, and that reminds me, will you telephone Orthodontics, ask if they know when the Oral Surgeon, Mr Harrison, will be coming. It should be today, but I'd like an approximate time.'

I said 'yes' to everything, it seemed the easiest way. I made the phone call, dealt with two others, and was reaching for my notebook, when the faint squeak of tyred wheels, and the jolting chink of crockery, meant that the big luncheon trolley had come. I saw the learner nurse thank the porter and tug it into the ward. So once more I left the office, I was hardly ever in it, I was like a bee always absent from the hive.

But being on the ward pleased me. I felt I was in my right place. I enjoyed walking from bed to bed, having a word with the patients, checking each meal with the detailed list in my hand. One or two patients ate in the day room up at a family table, but most were in bed, confined by weights, and pulleys, and plasters, and splints. As I ticked them all off on the list I recorded them in my mind; the spinal case just inside the doors, the fractured mandible opposite, the three fractured femurs on the right-hand side, then the mid-thigh amputee, the cracked pelvis, the acute disc lesion, the total hip replacement, the arthroplasty; I felt I knew them all.

When I came out it was nearly one, and the nursing shift was changing. Sister was giving out the report to the Staff Nurse taking her place. And I was supposed to be meeting Miss Reenham. I dragged a comb through my hair, washed my hands, and reached for my shoulder-bag. The lift, which was packed full like a bus, bore me up to Level 12, where Miss Reenham, still looking austere (and peeled without her white coat) beckoned me over to the queue at the serving hatch:

'How have you been getting on?' she asked, when with food collected, we found a vacant table and sat down.

I unwrapped my cutlery, choosing my words: 'On the whole, not bad,' I said.

'Of course, you're not a trained secretary, are you?' She poked at her salad, and scraped her lettuce before she took a bite.

'That's true, I'm not,' I passed her the salt, 'but I'm used to clerical work.' And how many *more* times, I thought, do I have to keep saying that—defending myself against these heavy odds.

'I told Sir John that you'd find it strange, and I wondered how Filey would be. She and Mayling had a girl lined up—a secretary from the agency. They were both keen as mustard to have her, but Sir John put a stop to it. He overrode them, *as is his right*, I'm not disputing that.' Miss Reenham was loyal, or being careful; she was also one of life's stirrers, a maker-of-waves, I had met her type before. She had summed me up, I was quite sure, and was very well aware that I'd hate to be the cause of any argument or discord, especially between

Uncle and his staff. In other words, she had told me on purpose. I had seen the snap of her eyes before she bent them down to her lettuce again.

'Blood's thicker than water,' I said, disliking the expression, but using it with blunt deliberateness. 'I dare say I start with a disadvantage, being Sir John's niece, but I need a job for the same reasons as most other people do, for the interest of being occupied, for the satisfaction it gives, and for the money too. I've a London rent to meet.'

'So long as you know what you're up against,' her long cheeks went mottled. I wished I hadn't been quite so sharp with her. And I was up against far more than she knew, I reflected unhappily. I was up against James Mayling's first impression of me in the train. He would never forgive me for denigrating his sons.

'That accident you were in, it must have been simply terrible,' she was changing tack. Perhaps she thought it best.

'Yes, it was,' I said briefly, 'and my time in hospital seemed to go on for ever.'

'I don't suppose Eileen Frewin will like it much, either. She was admitted yesterday, you know. She's in Gynae, Abbotts Ward.'

'Oh, really,' I reached for my yoghourt, and peeled off the tin-foil lid.

'She's in for a hysterectomy, she has the op tomorrow. Mayling's bound to visit her, and Sir John too, I should think. She's been here years, even longer than I, and I came in fifty-four.'

'That's a long time ago.'

'Before you were born,' Miss Reenham actually smiled. 'It was before the tower block was built. We were housed in the main building then.' She went on to tell me a little about the history of St Stephen's. I was glad the talk had got on to impersonal lines.

I studied her carefully as she talked, noting the permed grey hair, which was dressed in a sort of tea-cosy style, with nothing behind the ears. The bright blue eyes (when not flashing) were cold, and her lipstick didn't suit her. Yet she wasn't bad looking, and she could have been handsome in a slightly horsey way. Her expression spoiled her, all her muscles looked clamped, as though she couldn't let go. She was malicious, not much, perhaps, but malice is hard to hide. It spoils the face and etches nasty lines. I knew she wasn't the sort of person I would want to turn to for help, and I had an idea that the wide parquet landing running between our two wards would remain uncrossed, so far as I was concerned. If I went to Miss Reenham for help, she would gloat, she would say, 'I told you so'. Oh, not in so many words to my face, but to others behind my back. She would be pleasant to me, up to a point, because it behoved her to be. She would be pleasant because I was Uncle John's niece, and she'd not want to fall from grace. 'I was only too glad to help her, Sir John,' . . . I could hear her saying that—except that I didn't intend to give her the chance.

But how I wished there was someone to turn to when, back in the office again, I was trying my hardest to get my letters typed. I managed the discharge reports all right, for the case-notes helped me with those, all the relevant data was set out. But the letters were something else again, they were conversational, they were doctor-to-doctor, the sentences wouldn't link up. I was going to fail, I looked in dismay at my scrawled shorthand outlines. There they sat, looping and swooping, and they didn't mean a thing. They just sat there meaning nothing, absolutely nothing. I looked, and puzzled, I peered at them sideways, I held my book up to the light, I looked at them through a magnifying glass that I found in the desk drawer. I still couldn't read them. I was falling down on the job.

Three o'clock struck and visiting started, the corridor buzzed with people. Through into the ward they went with their flowers, and fruit, and sweets, and bottles of squash, and magazines and books. On a wave of irritation I got up and closed the door. Not that this made any difference, I still couldn't read my outlines, couldn't 'translate' them, and I simply dared not guess. With James Mayling guessing was out. It simply wouldn't work. He would know precisely word-for-word what he had dictated. If I improvised he'd be on to it in a flash.

I went to the window for a little air. I cooled my head on the pane. Down in the street strolled carefree people, the afternoon was warm; a coach-load of trippers were making their way to the beach. There was only one thing for me to do, and that was confess to James Mayling. I must ask him to re-dictate his letters, and offer to stay on late, admit that he went a little too fast for me. After all, what could he do? Nothing very much. But that wasn't the point. I hated the thought of it.

The telephone rang, I turned to answer it: 'Lytton Ward, this is the office.'

'Is that Miss Westering?' The voice was female and sounded near at hand.

'Thea Westering speaking, but who . . .'

'Oh, Miss Westering, this is Eileen Frewin, the

woman whose job you're doing, you know. I'm speaking from Abbotts Ward.'

'Why yes, hello.' She sounded nice, I wondered why she'd rung.

'Look, don't think I'm interfering,' she continued, 'but how are you getting on? I wondered if there was anything I could help you with, or explain. I tried to leave everything just so, but well, you know how it is. I've been lying here thinking, going over it all, and I've thought of several more things. I suppose . . .' she stopped speaking for a second, and faintly from her end I could hear the muted sounds of Abbotts Ward. 'I suppose,' she was sounding a little doubtful, 'I suppose you couldn't come up? I've no visitors this afternoon, and I'd so much like to meet you. Of course, if you're busy . . .'

The receiver slipped, and I grabbed at it feverishly. Had I heard aright, had she really said . . . had she actually offered *to help*? For a minute my voice deserted me, then it came back in a croak: 'Mrs Frewin, I'm not busy, well, actually, I *am*, but I'm in a terrible spot as well. I can't make sense of my letters—Mr Mayling's letters, and I'm going up the wall!'

'Come and see me,' her response was immediate, 'come up with your book, bring any other attaching papers, we'll sort them out between us. Take your tea break now, that'll give us time. I'm in bed number twenty-six.'

'But . . . are you sure?' Guilt rushed in, the poor woman was ill. And me a nurse, and bothering a patient, the absolute cardinal sin.

'Believe me, I couldn't be more sure. Think what you'll do for my ego. I'll feel indispensable, won't I, a truly heady feeling, practically as good as a shot in the arm!'

She sounded fun, as well as nice, I thought, as I gathered my papers, and walked up two flights of stairs to level six. Abbots Ward, like Lytton, was awash with visitors. I picked out Mrs Frewin as the patient on her own. She was sitting up in bed in a glamorous strappy nightie, looking a little anxiously at the doors. She was one of those women whom magazines describe as fresh-as-a-daisy. She was middle-aged, with a pink and white skin, a thin oval face, big eyes under a thick blonde fringe. I liked the look of her very much, her smile was friendly and open. One of Father's crime novels lay on her bed.

'I warned off all visitors today, now, of course, I feel lonesome,' she said, once I was settled by her bed.

'Your operation's tomorrow, I believe?'

'Tomorrow's the big day. As from midnight no food will pass my lips! I'll be glad when it's over, of course, but everyone says that. Still, never mind about me, I'm so glad you've come up. Shall we look at those letters, and try to straighten them out?'

They were straightened out so easily that I felt a positive fraud. But reading them over to Eileen seemed to clear my head, or stimulate memory, and most of the blanks I was able to fill in myself. 'You see, you'd got the main part right, there was only a word or two needed,' she smiled at me as I snapped my notebook shut.

'Yes, I dare say, but that word or two made all the difference,' I said. 'You've saved me making an idiot of myself.'

'With James?'

'Yes.'

'How did you find him, apart from his rapid dictation?'

'We-ell . . .' I hesitated, then decided to tell the truth. I told her about our meeting in the train.

'Oh dear!' she laughed a little, but was sympathetic too. 'He's a very fair-minded man, Thea. He wouldn't hold it against you. The thing is he dotes on the twins, which is natural, of course. And I happen to know that his last housekeeper has just given notice, so things are maybe a little rocky at home.'

'Is he divorced?'

'Good heavens, no, whoever told you that? Valerie Mayling died, poor girl, of acute meningitis. She took ill out in South Africa, whilst visiting her parents. They didn't get help soon enough, didn't recognise her symptoms. When they did, it was too late for the drugs to work.'

'How long ago?'

'Two years. The twins were only four. Mrs Mayling (James's mother) closed up her house in Cornwall, and came to live with him for a time, for about six months, I think. He got a housekeeper eventually, and Mrs Mayling moved, sold her house in Cornwall and bought one in West Lowhampton. She's got a sister there, a single woman, owns a small hotel. Mrs M's been widowed for some years. I rather think she's back with James now, till he gets fixed up again. It's not so easy to find a housekeeper, not where there are children. All in all, James has had a lot to bear.'

'I see, yes.'

'Still, I'm sure you know he's engaged to Sister Filey. Ruth's a natural home-making type, and she gets on well with the twins. She'll find it a wrench to give up nursing, she's incredibly efficient. She was a Ward Sister when she was twenty-five.'

'Here at St Stephen's?'

'No, somewhere in Kent. She's only been here a year. She and James got engaged at Christmas. An autumn wedding's planned, or so I believe.' She broke off, as she saw me reach for my files. 'I'm holding you up. I can see you're dying to make a start on those letters.'

'Well, I think perhaps I should,' I said, I took my chair back to the table. 'I can't thank you enough for your help,' I returned and shook her hand.

'I did very little, as well you know. Come and see me again. Come up towards the end of the week, when I'm off all drips and tubes, and feeling spry, and more myself again!'

I promised I would, I wished her luck, I made my way to the doors, dodging round groups of visitors coming in. The corridor was nearly deserted: nearly, but not quite, for coming through the doors from the landing, and looking straight at me was Mr Mayling . . . was James Mayling. I simply couldn't believe it, I couldn't believe I could have that much bad luck. My steps lagged, but his didn't; we met by the ward doors; he was carrying a sheaf of tulips wrapped in tissue paper; the tissue rattled as he stopped in front of me.

'You're a long way from home?' He looked mystified, then I saw his eyes go to my notebook. I wasn't trying to hide it, I just hoped that he might not see it. A vain hope; his puzzled look increased. 'Why are you walking around with these?' he indicated the notebook and the papers and files I'd stuck between its leaves.

'I've been to see Mrs Frewin.'

'Is she a friend of yours?'

He must have known she wasn't, I had no need to shake my head. But looking at him, up at him, I saw his expression change, a kind of dawning realisation made pinpoints of his eyes; they narrowed and sharpened, they looked like snippets of steel: 'You've not been pestering her with *work*?' Incredulity sat on his face . . . he looked almost shocked. My heart sank down to my boots. '*Have* you?' he demanded.

His hectoring tone jarred, and made me angry. I found my voice at last: 'Mrs Frewin rang down to the office to ask if I was all right. She asked if there was anything she could help me with, and as it happened there was. I couldn't read part of my shorthand. You went too fast for me.'

'I asked if you wanted to check anything!'

'I know, but I didn't like ... .'

'Instead you brought work right up here, worried a patient in bed!'

'I don't think I worried her,' I said defensively, but my voice lacked conviction, I knew it did, I was feeling guilty again.

He pushed past me, and opened the doors; I stood there against the wall: 'I don't think I've ever heard anything like it, in all my *life*!' he said. He turned round with one hand on the door, the other holding his flowers, and just for a second, even in that heated, angry second, I saw that he had a look of his small son, William, clutching his primroses in the train. But then he was through, and the doors closed, and all I could see of him was his head and shoulders through the glass portholes, swinging away from me, moving towards Eileen Frewin's bed.

Back on the Unit I sandwiched paper and carbon

together, rolled it into my typewriter and began. I typed with trembling fingers, I felt angry and contrite, mortified too, at having been caught out. But it was no good dwelling on it, the least I could do now was make sure every letter was perfect, I must concentrate on that. He would come down here at five o'clock and tell me off, of course. Of that I was quite, quite sure; he had hardly begun upstairs. Upstairs had been little more than the absolute tip of his wrath. There was more to come; he wasn't the sort to let me off lightly, on account of my being related to his Chief.

I typed and typed, and all went well, the afternoon wore on. I could hear people passing by in the corridor, cups chinking in the kitchen, the small ward kitchen three doors away from me. I had finished my very last letter and was reading it carefully through, when a curly head of carrotty brilliance came round my door, and a pert voice asked if I'd like some tea.

'I'd love some,' I said. The girl was the Staff Nurse I'd seen signing on at lunchtime, the one who had taken Sister Filey's place.

'It's through in the kitchen,' she led the way, cap perched high on her curls. 'We're not supposed to brew up in here, not for ourselves,' she said, 'but rules are made to be broken, aren't they, or at any rate some of them are. You're Miss Westerling, aren't you, Sir John's niece?'

I told her that I was. She poured two cups of near-black tea from a pot on the draining-board. 'I heard you typing like crazy,' she said, 'I looked in once or twice, but you didn't see me. I'm Susan Cater,' she helped herself to sugar, came to the table, stirring busily.

We drank in silence for a minute or two. I was grateful for the tea: 'It's saved my life,' I told her.

'I thought you looked fraught,' she smiled. She had light green eyes, she was snub-featured, she was round about my age: 'Makes it awkward, doesn't it,' she said, 'you're being Sir's niece . . . not for me, I don't give a monkey's, but you must know what I mean. There are those who'll avoid you, and those who'll suck up, and those who'll put on an act. You'll never know who your friends are, will you?'

'I expect I'll find out,' I replied. I sounded tart, and I knew I did; for I knew she spoke the truth. But I'd heard that particular refrain before, coming from Wendy's lips. Susan wasn't unlike Wendy, she had the same blunt manner, but at least she had approached me, made friendly overtures. She had also, it seemed, found me a white coat.

Back in the office I tried it on, Susan circling round me: 'I thought so, it's the right size,' round she went again: 'It suits you, goes with black hair, and I like the belt at the back. It's one of the new American sort, we've only just got them in.'

I liked it too, I felt better inside it—more efficient and *armoured*. There was nothing like looking the part; I would be ready for James Mayling when he came in at five to sign his mail.

He came in exactly on the hour. The church clock in Abbey Road was busily striking, as he sauntered through my door: 'Are my letters ready?' He sat down at the kneehole side of the desk. I had been standing, closing the window, when he arrived.

'Yes, they're here,' I gave him the folder. He pushed my machine to one side, thanked me briefly, his eyes

meeting mine in a searching kind of sweep, as he un-
snapped a ballpoint from his coat.

I found myself holding my breath as he opened the
folder, read the first letter, signed it, and started on the
next. One okay, six to go, and then the discharge
reports. I could hear my watch ticking, I could hear my
heart beating, I could hear the sound of his breathing,
the scrape of his sleeve across the polished desk. He had
strong wrists, narrow hands, long tapering fingers. Only
two more letters to go, he would soon be on the reports.
And so far, so good, there were no mistakes, not one. I
could glean nothing from his face, for little of it was
visible—just a foreshortened view of brow, nose, and
thick curling lashes, flickering slightly against his wind-
tanned cheeks. Did he sail, I wondered, was that where
he got that glowing, weathered look?

'Yes, they're fine,' his voice and the snapping shut of
the cardboard folder made me jerk in my chair and
swallow convulsively. 'Next time perhaps you could clip
the appropriate envelope on to each letter, saves any
possible error.' He handed me the folder, stood up and
politely wished me goodnight.

And then he was gone, and gone so quickly, it was like
a disappearance. One minute he was there, the next I
was watching the door close behind him. The anticipated
telling-off hadn't materialised. And yet I had felt he was
brimming with it, had been bursting to let fly. I had
sensed it in him, banked down in him, beating its wings
to escape. But he'd said not a word, not a single word; I
could only feel relief, and I guessed that Eileen Frewin
had intervened. She had probably made him promise
. . . had *asked* him to let things be, when he'd marched
to her bedside, breathing fire, saying he'd bumped into

me. And I didn't know whether I was glad of this, for I liked to fight my own battles. I always felt that nothing was solved by brushing it under the carpet; it was apt to come out later on in some other form or guise. Still, she'd meant well, and he'd held his tongue, and signed every single letter . . .

What more did I want? Certainly not a row.

CHAPTER THREE

OVER THE following two weeks I settled into the job, and although I enjoyed many facets of it, I still longed to nurse. The feeling was strong as a torrent in me, so strong that there were times when I felt I must go on to the ward to adjust a patient's pillows, or change a drip, or do a dressing, irrigate a mouth, help turn a patient, give the medicines out. But of course I didn't, it wasn't my place, I would watch it all going on through my viewing window, and envy the others, and curse my wretched knee. I would feel like a nurse waiting in the wings.

I continued to type for James Mayling, of course, whenever the need arose. He would come strolling into my room, clicking the door to behind him, appropriating the whole of my desk, littering it with notes. He would say, 'Good morning', remark on the day, sit yourself down and begin, his white coat crinkled up at the hem. Since my first day he had taken good care to dictate more slowly. In a way I was glad, in a way I was not, for I felt he was humouring me. I wanted to do the job as it was, as Eileen Frewin had done it. I didn't want it made easier for me, at least not to that extent. He even spelled out simple words, ordinary words like 'bladder'. I longed to tell him he needn't bother, but something always stopped me—a gleam of amusement in his eye, laughter at my chagrin? Was it there? Did I imagine it? I could never be quite sure. All I knew was I daren't draw his fire, I was *careful* in his presence. And I never really relaxed until he had gone.

Then one Sunday morning I met him on the sea-front. It was early, not eight o'clock, he had the children with him. I had gone out to walk and think, for Hugh was coming that day. He had rung up the night before, he would be at The Moorings for lunch. I felt a little twitchy about it, I felt a walk might help. So I had gone out with my head full of Hugh, and had seen James Mayling rounding the corner, flanked by his sons and a dog.

I was in emerald green culottes and top, so he couldn't fail to see me, especially as we had the Undercliff Walk to ourselves. There was hardly anyone else in sight, apart from one or two anglers digging for sandworms down at the water's edge.

The little dog, a Jack Russell terrier, with a tan patch over one eye, reached me first, wagging his stump of tail. His patch gave him the look of having a cap on the side of his head. He barked and pranced, front legs down, rear and tail raised high. 'Good morning!' James Mayling called. He was several paces away, casually dressed in lightweight slacks and a blue open-neck shirt. He introduced the two children, who I didn't think recognised me—a fortnight is a long time in the life of a six-year-old. They were very correct and shook hands solemnly. 'Glorious day, going to be warm. We must make the most of it,' their father said, preparing to walk on.

Our meeting would, therefore, have been of the briefest, if the little terrier dog hadn't suddenly made up his mind to run back and jump up. Dogs are my weakness, I can never resist them, and this one was a beaut. I sank down on my heels and stroked his narrow bone-hard head, and quivering body, and velvet-soft envelope ears. At a shout of: 'Badger, come here at once,' from one of the little boys, he was off to join his family, without a backward glance. I could hear the scratch of his nails as he scampered away.

And as for me, I was in a spot. I struggled to rise and could not. I had forgotten my right knee's limitations, I couldn't spring up from my heels. To get to my feet I would have to lean sideways, take the weight on my other leg, and push myself up with a thrust of my arms. Even that would be difficult. Well, for heaven's sake, what a fool I was to put myself in this position. And I cursed even more when, in swivelling sideways, my bad knee gave a twinge, and I gasped in fright, and measured my length on the ground. At first I could only think of my knee. Had I damaged it? I was too scared to move for a second, then I heard the sound of footsteps, saw feet, one on each side of me, long straddled legs, then hands coming down and lifting me up, gripping me under the armpits, remaining there, holding me up like a doll.

'Are you hurt?'

'No.'

James Mayling's face looked intently into mine.

'I'm all right now,' I assured him quickly, but he didn't let me go. He gave a kind of shake to his head:

'I'll get you to the wall.'

He meant the sea wall, which was very near. I could have hopped there myself, but he gave me no chance, he turned me sideways, grasped me round the waist: 'All right, now . . . off we go.' It was like a three-legged race, his two legs and my one; he sat me down on the wall. It was low and broad and made of concrete, rounded and smooth on top; he knelt in front of me, had a good look at my knee. 'Straighten it out, now bend up.' His fingers

were round my ankle, gently pushing my heel back to my
thigh: 'Does it hurt . . . any pain?'

'No, none at all.'

'Then you haven't done any damage.' He got up and
sat on the wall at my side, and turned round to face me:
'You know, Thea, I don't think,' he said, and his long
mouth quirked, 'that you're really quite ready to
attempt a knees-bend at this stage of your recovery!'

'I know, I know, it was stupid of me!' I moved, and our
shoulders touched, 'but sometimes it's quite all right,
you know, I can get away with it. Sometimes I have
trouble in starting and stopping, if I try to run, that is.' I
was gabbling, and I knew I was. His nearness was
overwhelming, overpowering. I didn't know where to
look.

'That's common after a patellectomy. You should
know that, being a nurse.'

'I do know it.' My hair blew forward, screening me
from him. Our conversation ground to a standstill, and
petrified by the silence I felt nothing less than grateful to
the children, who came rushing up from the beach.

'Daddie, have you got Badger's ball?' Barty asked,
staring at me. His father produced a tennis ball out of his
trousers pocket. Then both boys were off again, pushing
one another and giggling. We heard the clash of their
feet on the shingle below.

'They're getting out of hand,' James said. 'I'm not
with them nearly enough.' We watched them race to the
hard-ribbed sand, they were throwing the ball for
Badger; the still air echoed with his barks. It was a
perfect morning of brilliant colours—azure, green and
silver, diamond-bright where the sun's rays hit the sea.
The cliff face rose up stark and white, pitted with

hand-sized caves, where the grey and white gulls, called kittiwakes, had their nests. From the mouth of the natural harbour streamed lines of little yachts. The man beside me was watching them, his face was turned from me; I stared at the column of his throat, and fought for words to say.

'You live in the village, don't you,' I managed. I knew he did, of course. Aunt Meg had pointed his house out to me—two cottages knocked into one, grey stone, with a thatched roof, and a garden full of lilacs, or so it had seemed to me as we'd driven past.

'At Northbarn, yes, I'm attached to it.' His face came round to mine. 'But my domestics don't seem to be, they all want to live in the town. The last one has just left me—the third in eighteen months. It's a pretty trying state of affairs, especially for my mother, who comes in at the double to fill the breach. She's with me now, which isn't ideal, for all sorts of reasons.' He sighed, and turned, and looked over the wall at the boys. 'I suppose you live in the nurses' home in London, do you?' he asked.

I shook my head: 'No, not now,' I said, 'I have my own flat. I share it with another nurse. It's better than living in.'

'Are you missing your friends?'

'Down here you mean? Well, yes, of course I am. I expected to. That's part of it, but four months will soon pass. Two weeks have gone already,' I smiled, but he didn't respond.

'Counting the days, are you?' he said, and his cynical look returned. What a prickly man he was, I thought, how easy to offend. He wasn't much like a man in love, for the 'in love' state is a softener, a happy-making state when one feels completely in tune with the world, and ready to smile at one's very worst enemy.

The children returned at that point, making their usual din. William was examining a skein of bladderwrack brought up from the breakwater, Barty was pulling the ball from Badger's jaws.

'Ready for breakfast, you two?' James ruffled William's hair. Both children wore butcher-blue shorts and blue-and-white-striped T-shirts. Barty's hair was darker than William's, more tawny gold, like his father's. I observed the difference. William looked at me and smiled:

'It's Daddie's Sunday off,' he said, 'we're going to do something *special*.'

'But we can't go sailing, it makes Ruth sick!' Barty mimed hideously.

'We might go up in an aeroplane,' William followed the progress of a small trainer-plane limping into the sky.

'Don't be silly, William. You know we won't. Isn't he silly, Dad?' Barty was scathing, and he didn't pull his punches—just like his father again. He turned to me, pointing upwards: 'I think you live up there, in that big house with the red roof on the cliff.'

'I'm staying there, just for the summer, Barty.'

'We've been there with Nan. She's friends with the lady who makes all the jam, and she's got a big tortoise, as big as that.' He spread his hands out wide.

'The lady's my aunt.'

'Oh, *is* she? We've got an aunt as well. She lives in a house called Nash, and it's a hotel inside, and people stay there, and . . .'

'Come on, you two,' their father interrupted, 'we'll

sprint along to the harbour and back, and then get home to breakfast.'

I got up too, and although he watched me, he offered no assistance. Not that I needed it, I was quite all right. We said goodbye at the ramp. I was half-way up it when I heard William's voice echoing up from the path: 'Daddie . . . that lady . . . *do* you know who she is? She's the cross lady who shouted in the train!' His father said something in reply, but by then I was out of range. Heavens, I thought, what a reputation to get.

'Helen Mayling,' Aunt Meg told me later, as she put the roast in the oven, 'is autocratic, but an absolute sweetie at heart. She's back at Northbarn, helping James out, looking after the boys. He's going all out to find another housekeeper, poor man, but they none of them want to live that far out, unless they're elderly, and elderlies tend to baulk at little boys. It's a good thing he's getting married. It's the best solution there is. Helen will rest easy then, and not keep worrying. She's got a sister, you know, Ann Fellowes, who lives in the town. She's got one of those elegant Nash houses right on the front. She's turned it into a small hotel and is doing very well. Oh Thea,' her voice changed, 'watch your skirt on that table. You don't want to spot it,' she elbowed me out of the way. I had changed my culottes for a cotton flounced skirt in brilliant cerise, and a white blouse with a ruffle round the neck. All for Hugh . . . all for Hugh? Well, not exactly, perhaps. There was no reason, though, why I shouldn't look my best.

'I suppose Ruth Filey and James will live at Northbarn when they're married?' The name, James, came easily to me. I felt it suited him. He looked like a James, I said it again in my head.

'Presumably, yes. I don't really know,' Aunt Meg answered my query. 'Ruth's got a flat near the hospital. I suppose they might live there, except that it wouldn't be ideal for the boys.'

'You know her, don't you? What do you think of her?' I don't know why I asked, except that I'd never quite been able to make up my mind about Ruth. In her quiet way, she was managing, I thought, but perhaps most Sisters were, and I'd never met her off the ward, so who was I to judge?

'Oh, I like her,' Aunt Meg said, cutting a melon in half, 'but I take people at their face value, you know, I can't be bothered with depths. Your uncle's the same, we're not critical, life's too short for that.' She put the melon in the fridge, wiped her hands on her apron, 'Hugh prefers cheese to a pudding. You won't mind, just this once?'

'I like cheese too,' I said, going out into the garden. I knew she wouldn't want any help, she enjoyed preparing food. She even enjoyed doing household chores, and had very little assistance, apart from a cleaner, who came in twice a week.

Uncle John was in the garden, supine on a chair-bed— a mound of yellow in his tight new cardigan, his face turned up to the sky; he passed me the paper as I took the other chair. I kept very quiet, he wanted to doze, and I think he managed it, for when a car turned into the drive, making the gravel spit, he didn't stir; it was I who shot to my feet. Hugh, I thought it was bound to be Hugh. The wing of the house hid the car, and its occupant; I waited on the lawn. The car door slammed, I heard gravelly footsteps, voices inside the house. Then out he came, and yes, it was Hugh, running lightly down the steps, snappily dressed in a striped blazer, light trousers and dark brown shirt. The face above the knotted cravat was smiling and confident, then my feet took me forward, I found my hands in his:

'Little Thea grown up!'

'Not so little,' I laughed.

'But very beautiful,' he leaned forward and kissed me. Our height was exactly the same. We linked arms and moved to the chairs. Uncle John greeted Hugh. 'I'll leave you two to talk,' he said, and off he went to the house, his slippers flapping, his cardigan riding up.

'I couldn't believe you were here for the summer,' Hugh's fingers touched my wrist.

'I couldn't believe you were in Lowhampton.'

'We lost touch,' he said. And he said it with a reproachful air, for all the world, I thought, as though it was me who had made those promises five years ago, and had broken them too. Really, men were the absolute end.

Nevertheless, sitting there with my hand rolled inside his, I knew I was pleased to see him, knew I was glad he was back. And looking at him, listening to him (we talked for a very long time) I had that feeling common to friends who meet after several years, a feeling of affectionate recognition, a feeling of 'yes, of course', as expressions, and gestures and mannerisms are remembered all over again, and surprise is felt at having forgotten them. I rather thought he felt the same, that the feeling was mutual. So in a way our time apart came together again, with a single snap, as though it had never been.

Over lunch he told us all about his trip to Exeter. 'I got most of the stuff I wanted,' he said, 'I was only outbid once. There's a piece of Chelsea you might like, Meg' (he never called her Aunt). 'It's small, about this big,' he held up his fork, 'eighteenth century, a man on horseback, I'll keep it till you've seen it.' He named a price that made me gasp, but Aunt Meg appeared untroubled:

'Bring it next time you've over here, darling,' she said.

'I never thought you'd leave Elverstein's,' I said later on, when at Hugh's suggestion we went down to the beach.

'There was no chance of making such headway with them,' he smiled at me easily. 'My contract was running out, so it seemed a good time to break. I was lucky to meet up with Carl when I was here last autumn. I've always wanted a partnership and one day he'll retire. I shall change the name then to Delter Antiques, or even Delter and Son! Now, *that's* something to plan for,' he tossed a pebble and caught it. His face turned to mine, his expression was hard to read.

'So,' I said, teasing him, 'marriage is part of your scheme.'

'Might be, you never know.'

'I'll believe that when it happens.' I was still laughing, but his face had changed, he turned round and kissed me, holding me fast when I made to draw away. Eventually he let me go, smoothing his hand down my hair:

'Little Thea, with the sleepy eyes and mouth so innocent, are you going to stay in London all your life?'

'Quite possibly, yes.' My voice shook. The kiss had been probing and deep, and ill-timed, and short on tenderness. He hadn't liked me drawing away, a thwarted Hugh could be rough; but it was my fault for teasing him, I ought to have had more sense than to lead

him on, however unwittingly. I scanned the beach,
scarcely seeing it; colours and people merged. Way
down by the water's edge a family were playing rounders; there were one or two hardy types swimming (the
sea was like ice until June); there were wind-surfers, and
skin divers, whilst out beyond the buoys a speedboat was
filling the air with a broken droning sound . . . whoo-
oomph . . . whoo-oomph . . . whoo-oomph . . . whoo-
oomph . . . its stern well down, its prow raised, stirring
the water to foam.

'I suppose you know several people down here?'
Hugh took his blazer off, rolled it into a pillow, and lay
down.

'Not really,' I said, 'but last weekend I had a friend
down from London—Wendy Shaw, my flatmate. It was
great to have her there.'

My skirt blew back against his hand, he fingered the
scalloped hem: 'So you're not shacked up with a boy-
friend.' His eyes were tightly closed. I watched his
mouth moving beneath the black moustache.

'No, I'm not.'

'I thought most girls . . .' he began, but I cut him off:

'It's a mistake to generalise, Hugh,' I said, trying to
keep my voice light.

'But being a nurse.'

'Nurses are exactly the same as other people . . . some
do and some don't, and there the matter ends.'

'Sorry.'

'No need to be.'

'Thea, look at me,' I felt him tugging at my arm, but I
really hardly noticed, for a group of people by the
breakwater caught and held my eye. It was the family
who'd been playing rounders, the man was carrying the

bat, and yes, it was James, followed by Ruth, followed
by William and Barty. They were all laughing and
scrambling over the rocks. I stared at them, and how
could I, I thought, not have known them at once. But
they looked so different—he in shorts, she in a one-piece
swimsuit. I didn't want to meet them, not now, not here.
Oh, why had they chosen *this* beach. In a flutter of
confusion my hand went up to my hair. It was then that
Ruth saw me, she looked across and waved. I waved
back and got to my feet, I was motivated by habit, for
one always stood up for a Sister, even one on the beach,
even one off-duty on the arm of a Registrar—the sight of
whom made my legs go weak. I was aware of Hugh's
startled: 'Who is it?' as he clambered up beside me; then
we all met, introductions got under way.

'I thought most ward sisters were dragons,' Hugh said,
shaking Ruth's hand.

'Hugh has preconceived ideas about the nursing profession,' I put in quickly, stealing a glance at James. His
expression, as always, was hard to read, then his slow
smile came, broadening his face, deepening the lines at
the corners of his mouth:

'How's the knee?' he asked me.

'Perfectly all right.'

'Swimming won't hurt it, you know. Hydro-therapy's
just the job, but wait until the water's warmer, or go to
the local baths.'

'There's nothing wrong with the water today,' Ruth
was climbing into her skirt, 'but he chickened out, Thea
. . . there's men for you!'

'Ruth's a toughie,' he said. He bent down to Barty,
cleaning a smudge off his cheek. The little boy leaned
against his father and cast an eye round at me.

'We can both swim,' he told me, 'but Nannie said not today. She said we'd got to wait until Whitsun, so Dad and I dug a moat all the time that Ruth was in the sea.'

'And we're having our tea down here on a cloth. Nan's bringing it,' William said, giving his glasses a shove. His remark, coming then, made us all laugh. Even Hugh said he was glad that the niceties of cloth were being observed.

'I think this is Nan now,' James said, and he went up the concrete steps to take a basket and two Thermos flasks from the hands of a plumpish lady in a green blouse and Black Watch tartan skirt. Once again there were introductions. Mrs Mayling and I shook hands.

'I've heard a great deal about you from your aunt,' she said to me. She was very formal, distant even. She wouldn't be easy to know. Her gaze was discerning, her eyes brown, she had a retroussé nose which saved her face from being censorious. Her glance passed from me to Hugh, stayed on him rather longer. 'So you're back in England, Mr Delter, *and* in the provinces. You'll find us a very drastic change from New York.'

'New York was the drastic part, Mrs Mayling.' I felt Hugh shift beside me, felt his arm about my shoulders: 'I'm glad to be back,' he said. He was acting, and I knew he was, but I didn't mind just then. I was glad of his presence, I felt paired off, as Ruth and James were paired. They were spreading the cloth, and weighting down the ends.

'Why not stay and have tea with us?' Mrs Mayling said, slicing a cake into wedges with a deft flick of her wrist. 'There's plenty to eat, and if we use the cups off the Thermos flasks . . .'

'Oh no,' I said quickly, 'it's kind of you, but Aunt Meg's expecting us back.'

'She is, actually.' Hugh was supportive, and again I was grateful to him. We said goodbye, and moved up the steps, leaving them sitting there, having their Sunday picnic on the beach.

'Hey, watch where you're putting your feet!' we heard James say. One of the twins was getting told off again.

'I suppose he's engaged to the pretty blonde piece,' Hugh said as we passed the shops, and made our way to the cliff and the drive of the house.

'He is, yes.'

'They look married already.'

I agreed with him that they did. 'And quite apart,' he continued, 'from her obvious physical charms, she's good with his kids and seems to get on with her future ma-in-law.'

'I noticed that, yes.'

'So your Golden Goliath's got everything in his own ditch.'

'My Golden Goliath, as you call him,' I said, 'would probably have a wide choice. I can't see many girls turning him down, with or without his children.'

'Not fallen for him yourself, have you?'

'Not so you'd notice,' I laughed. And now it was my turn to put on an act. 'And even if I had, even if I were bewitched by him, it wouldn't do any harm. I've discovered a lot about myself since you and I met last. I can fall in love at the drop of a hat, and as easily out again, with no hard feelings on either side.'

'Difficult to achieve that, the no hard feelings part.' We had reached the drive, and he drew me back against the tamarisk hedge. I went stiff as a board, but I needn't have worried, for his kiss was light and swift, as swift as the sunshine that needled its way through the trees: 'I'm not as vain as I was,' he said, touching the ends of my hair, 'I can read the keep-off signals. I don't usually blunder, Thea.'

'Oh Hugh, it's not . . .'

'I'd just like us to meet, to go out together occasionally. We've got the whole summer in front of us. I promise to behave.' His eyes were brown, his look was earnest, something stirred in me then. I wasn't completely immune to him, I was fond of him, I knew. Hugh was still Hugh, and here we were, together once again, in the garden of The Moorings, where once we had fallen in love.

I agreed to meet him, and as I did so I heard a warning bell clang . . . it clanged and banged itself out in my head . . . I ignored it, didn't heed it . . . which was foolish of me . . .

For perhaps I should have done.

CHAPTER FOUR

JAMES MAYLING'S Sunday off appeared to have done very little for him. He looked out of sorts and ragged tempered when he came on the ward on Monday. He was late, too, it was nearly midday, but I knew he had been in Theatre, helping with a new admission—a cervical spine dislocation. The patient had been returned to the ward and had just regained consciousness. I could see him through my viewing window, see the weights at the head of his bed, pulling down on the calipers drilled in his skull. He was a Mr Arthur Tell, a builder in the town. He had been in a car accident at the weekend.

I saw Ruth take James into the ward, and they did a short round. A few minutes later in he came to me. 'I want to do the discharge report on Martineau,' he said. He glanced at the cabinets and then at me, which meant he wanted the notes. I turned to get them, wary of his mood. 'It'd save time if you'd get the notes out before I arrive,' he said.

'I usually do,' I said pleasantly, placing the notes on the desk, 'but I hadn't realised you'd want to do Mr Martineau's report. He's not being discharged until three today.'

'I know that,' his chin jerked up, 'but I want to get it done.' He picked up the folder, opened it, then looked across at me: 'These aren't complete. The last blood count and ESR are missing.'

Oh no, I thought, caught out again. I dived for the

filing tray: 'I may not have filed them, they're probably here.' They were, and I snatched them up. I handed them to him. 'I'm very sorry,' I said.

He grunted, but didn't look pleased. He pinned the reports in the notes, pricked his thumb and swore volubly under his breath: 'All right, all right, let's get *on*!' He sounded furious; he began to dictate before I could open my book. He went fast too, much too fast. He dictated like that first time, on my first day, when I'd had to get help from Eileen. Well, I'd not get help from that quarter now, Eileen had been discharged. So I swallowed my pride and asked him to slow, I told him I couldn't keep up. I got a long look and a deep sigh in response: 'You mean I'm going too fast for you?'

'I'm afraid so, yes.'

'You surprise me. I thought I'd noticed, just very recently, a certain impatience with the way I dictated,' he said.

'You've gone from one extreme . . .' I began, but wasn't able to finish. He was off again, dictating again, but this time very slowly, so slowly that my pencil actually dragged. He was being perverse, deliberately awkward. What children men were, I thought. And how different he was from yesterday. Could it be the same man? I didn't like today's man, he made me feel tense and angry. My head was aching in little beats of pain. He finished at last, and I thought he would go. I certainly hoped he would, but he closed the folder of notes and just sat there, a deep frown drawing his brows:

'Martineau and Eileen Frewin are getting married,' he said, so suddenly and so out of context with all that had gone before, that I simply stared at him, saying nothing at all. 'They've known one another for donkey's years.'

He straightened two paper clips. 'They might have gone on like that till doomsday, then Martineau broke his leg. Eileen had to have surgery, and their simultaneous misfortunes seem to have had the effect of nudging them into the marriage-pot. He's a bachelor, she's a widow; there's nothing to stop them, of course.'

'Good for them. Who would want to stop it?' I found my voice at last.

'Did you know about it?' He looked suspicious.

'Not a whisper,' I said. 'Oh, I knew they liked one another, I couldn't help noticing that. He was always very anxious about her, and was often wheeled up to see her. I saw him there—in Abbotts Ward—twice when I visited, and she came down here to see him on Friday just before she went home. I thought they were very attached to each other, but I didn't think of marriage.'

'I heard last night,' he said, 'Eileen rang me at home. It's giving up her job that gets me, that really *is* a blow.'

'She's leaving?' I stared at him. I hadn't thought of that.

'Yes, she won't be coming back. She's sending in her notice. They're marrying at the end of September. He doesn't want her to work.'

'But won't she come back here at *all*?'

'I gather not,' he said, 'and precisely what that means is that Sister and I are going to have to get used to someone else.'

The realisation of what that meant struck home then. They would want to be settled, settled down with a permanent secretary. And I remembered what Miss Reenham had told me, in the canteen on my first day— about them once having found someone and having to let her go, because of me. And now, once again, I could be a stumbling block. In no way whatsoever was I having that.

'Naturally, I'll go,' I said, 'as soon as you've found a replacement. Filling in until the end of August doesn't apply any more. I'm sure you'll find someone very quickly, with jobs being so scarce.' My sentences came out very pat, and saying them brought relief, and disappointment, and anger as well; I almost felt let down. I felt miserable too, but I wouldn't admit to that.

'A helpful suggestion,' James Mayling said, completely poker-faced, 'but Sir John doesn't want the post advertised until just before you leave—until just before you are due to leave at the end of August. The original arrangement is not to be altered, he says.'

'I see,' I said with difficulty, thinking this one out. Couldn't he be . . . well, couldn't he be just a little warmer about it? Couldn't he say he was glad I'd be working my full term out? I wasn't such a dead loss in the office, there were some things I was good at. He was mean with praise. He was probably mean full-stop.

'That must be frustrating for you and Sister,' I managed to say at last. I loaded my words with sarcasm too, which wasn't lost on him.

'As a matter of fact it is,' he snapped. 'I don't like hanging about. I don't like temporary arrangements at all, I never think they work. I'd like to tackle the matter now and get a good permanent girl. I know Sister feels exactly the same, but we don't have the last word. Regrettably, we have to do as we're told.'

'Well, I don't,' I said distinctly, but he didn't appear to have heard me. There was a good deal of noise in the corridor.

'Sorry?' he inclined towards me.

I got up and went round the desk: 'I said, *I don't*, Mr Mayling. I can go or stay as I please. This job is only a filler for me, something for me to do. I wanted to do it, and finish it, because I promised I would. But the situation is different now, it's changed, and that lets me out.'

'Now, just a minute . . .' he got to his feet. We stood facing one another, very close, only inches apart. 'Before you go on . . .'

'I'd like to finish.' Nothing would stop me now, nothing, nothing would stop me now, I was burning and boiling inside. 'You've never been satisfied with what I do, you've made that very plain. Everyone else has been pleased and encouraging; they like me being here. But you, you've always had reservations and taken the trouble to show them. I don't like that. I happen to think it's rude!'

'Well, of all the outrageous . . .'

'It's true!'

'Don't be childish!' His face came down to mine, he gripped my arm and jerked me to him: 'I don't want you to go!' he said thickly, just as Ruth entered the room. She looked surprised and rather pale; her freckles were plain to see, so far as I could see anything in that blindingly angry moment. Through a kind of mist I heard her tell James that she'd heard us arguing right down the corridor near the sluice.

'A slight exaggeration, I think,' he said in his ice-chip voice, but I saw him move to stand over at her side. Two against one, I thought. And yes, of course, he was right, I *was* childish, shooting my mouth off, like that. 'Thea thinks she ought to leave,' he continued, and the last of my anger cooled. His use of my christian name, coming then, caused an annoying weakness. I could feel myself softening, giving in, I knew I wouldn't leave.

'Well, I hope you won't,' Ruth said, looking directly at me, with her spiky-lashed eyes, that were like a little girl's. 'It'll cause a shocking fuss if you do. James and I can do without that. I'm perfectly satisfied with your work, the patients and nursing staff like you. If it's just a matter of dictation, James, we could get over that if you'd only give in and put your work on a tape.'

'I'm not keen.'

'I know that, but in the circumstances .

'I'll think about it,' his voice was curt.

'It'd save such a lot of time. And you'd not need to trouble Thea, except when you come in to sign.'

My mouth dropped open, she'd got it all wrong: 'Good heavens, it's not any trouble!'

He flapped a hand and exasperation stamped itself over his face: 'All right, all right, for pity's sake! I'll use a dictating machine! I suppose you can audio-type?' he snapped, turning round to me.

'Yes I can. I've typed back tapes for my parents, on occasion.'

'There you are, James, couldn't be better.' Ruth's voice was meant to be soothing. 'Now, how about lunch? It's nearly one, and I'm just about to sign off. I'd like to go somewhere out in the town. I'm sick of this place this morning.'

They went out together, leaving me with my thoughts.

From then on things were different. In the office I had the tapes, a disembodied voice in my ear, instead of a large blonde man sitting within a few feet of me, painstakingly spelling out words. He still spelled them out on the tapes. Perhaps he thought I was mental—a stupid

girl whom his Chief had forced on him. Even so, he *had*
said that he didn't want me to leave, which was why I was
staying, in spite of everything.

There were very few changes on the ward, the patients
remained the same. But this was the case very often in an
orthopaedic ward. Generally speaking, ortho patients
are relatively long-term, for most fractures take several
weeks to mend. This was one of the main reasons why I
had gone in for bones. I welcomed the chance to get to
know the patients as individuals. Even here at St
Stephen's, where I wasn't a nurse, the same feelings
flowed, for I saw the patients in the early mornings when
I took round their personal mail, and again at lunchtimes
when I checked their diet sheets. There was always a
strong temptation to linger, and sometimes I did. I
would stop and rearrange the flowers, or tidy someone's
locker or (greatly daring) plump up a pillow or two.

Mr Tell, the patient with the injured neck, who had
been the last admission, was still on skull traction, but
progressing very well. Apart from disliking having to
suck his food through a plastic tube, he was cheerful and
didn't complain very much: 'They tell me I'll be into a
collar soon, just like a giraffe-necked woman,' he smiled
carefully, for movement was tricky; I put the container
of soup down on a stool (lower than his head) and put the
tube in his mouth. He sucked up a few mouthfuls, then
took the tube out again, 'It'll be great to be in a collar
and sitting up,' he said. 'Then I'll be on to solids,
Nurse—a nice bit of steak perhaps, or a cut off the joint,
with roast potatoes and greens.'

'You might get the greens, Mr Tell, but not the steak
and joint,' I laughed, just as Ruth appeared and whisked
me out of the ward. She had most likely heard him call

me 'Nurse' and not been overpleased. She liked her staff to be what they were, and to be addressed as such. She asked me to make out a requisition for a new ripple bed. Then she went on the ward and supervised lunches herself.

Even after a whole month I still hadn't got Ruth's measure. I felt she didn't show much of herself, that she played her cards close to her chest, but the following week, the following Wednesday, I saw her at her best. I saw her in action. I saw her save a life.

It was a stormy humid afternoon. She came on duty at one. All the lights were on in the Unit, outside it was nearly dark. Angry clouds, the colour of slate, were sitting down on the sea. There was sheet lightning, the thunder came in claps. I hated it, hated the atmosphere, I have always hated storms. I'm not exactly afraid of them, but I loathe the feeling they bring, like a kind of pressure on top of the skull, as though an unseen hand is trying to force one into the depths of the earth.

There were very few visitors when three o'clock came around. I saw one or two drip into the ward, their mackintoshes gleaming, umbrellas making rivers on the floor. I was just sipping a cup of tea brought in by Nurse Kyle, when a faint tap came on my door, and in walked Mrs Mayling (James' mother) in an oilskin and wellington boots.

'Good afternoon,' she crackled over, and stood by my desk, looking as though she had just come out of the sea.

'How nice to see you,' I said, rather startled, 'but what a dreadful day.'

'Appalling, and my car wouldn't start. I had a long wait for a bus.' She was very breathless. I hastily pulled up a chair.

'I've called to see Ruth.' She took the chair, and began to open her mack. 'I've looked in her room, but she's not there.'

'She's probably in the ward.' I glanced through, 'I'll tell her you're here.' I hurried to the door. Mrs Mayling was wiping her face on a handkerchief.

'I think I know what she's come about,' Ruth said, when I gave her the message. She walked slightly ahead of me, down the ward, not appearing to hurry, yet covering the ground with her usual noiseless speed. As we reached the last bed and turned to pass between the hooked-back doors, I heard her give a low exclamation, then saw the reason for it. Out in the corridor, lying face down, arms and legs spread wide, was Mrs Mayling, entirely motionless. I leapt forward, but Ruth was quicker. She was down on her knees in a second, turning her over, feeling for her pulse, striking the end of her breastbone, opening her mouth, glancing up at me: 'She's arrested. Dial 34 . . . Cardiac Team . . . hurry.' Then down went her head to the patient. I saw her breathe in her mouth. I raced to the phone and gave my message, I saw Susan join Ruth. By then my message was being relayed over the tannoy system: CARDIAC ARREST LYTTON WARD . . . CARDIAC ARREST LYTTON WARD. Ruth was inflating Mrs Mayling's lungs, Susan was thumping her chest, using the heels of her hands and working to Ruth's gasped-out instructions. I heard her say: 'Harder, harder, harder!' as I ran to fetch a bed-board. I knew they'd want that, the Team would want that; I found oxygen and a bag, and a laryngoscope; I hurried to Susan and Ruth. But the team were before me, they burst through the doors leading from the landing. There were three doctors and the big cumbersome cardiac trolley, which I knew would contain all the equipment they would need:

'Get that board on the bed in here,' one of the doctors yelled at me. He meant in the side-ward, I did what he said. They pushed everything out of the way, apart from the bed, which now had the board resting on top of the mattress. Mrs Mayling was all but flung on it; Ruth and Susan came in. I squeezed out and stood by the door, Mrs Mayling's clothes were cut off, an airway was tracked down her throat, oxygen connected, pumped into her lungs with an ambu-bag. A drip was set up, ECG leads were attached to each of her limbs. She was slippery with sweat, they had quite a job to get the leads to adhere. But presently, as I stood there, my own heart thundering hard, I heard the plaintive blip . . . blip . . . blip . . . blip . . . of the monitor, followed by a grunt and a shout from the young, bald doctor who straightened up, grinning from ear to ear:

'We have lift-off . . . she's in sinus rhythm!'

The anaesthetist looked at me: 'Ring Intensive Care, tell them to expect us in two minutes flat!' Already he was pulling the bed from the wall, marshalling his team. The third doctor called after me: 'And get a radiographer, we'll need a portable X-ray as soon as we reach ICU!'

I didn't answer. I just did what they said. And as I stood holding the phone, I could see the little procession rushing down the corridor. Susan was on one side, holding the drip, the anaesthetist on the other, squeezing the ambu-bag as he side-stepped along. Out through the doors they shot, the lift was waiting outside. I heard the crash of the lift gates, its whine as it left the floor. I sent up a prayer, I leaned against the wall. I knew, though, why they still had to rush, why they'd rush till they reached ICU. For the danger was that Helen Mayling could have another arrest, between wards, with probably fatal results.

I helped Nurse Kyle clear up the side-ward. I folded Mrs Mayling's clothes. A porter appeared and the resus trolley was wheeled back to its home, which was two floors down, in the main surgical wing. As I went back into my office I saw Ruth go into her room, heard her lift the telephone, ask for James to be bleeped. I went across and tapped at her door: 'Will she be all right, do you think?'

She shrugged, looked non-committal: 'That's any-body's guess. I'm just trying to get hold of James.' I saw her look at her watch. 'It's nearly four. The twins will have to be met out of school. Helen usually does it. I'll have to ring her sister, Ann Fellowes, at the hotel, I've got her number somewhere.'

'Would you like me to ring her?'

'No, I'll do it,' Ruth's hair was damp on her forehead. She looked exhausted. 'Thank you for helping,' she said.

A fat lot I did, I thought, as I sat at my desk. All I had done was fetch a board and rush about making calls. But Ruth, Ruth had saved Helen's life, had got respiration going, and heart massage started, before the team ar-rived. It was those first few minutes following an arrest that were absolutely crucial. Seconds count when a heart has ceased to beat. My cup and saucer were still on the sill. I'd been drinking tea, I remembered, when Helen Mayling had tapped and walked in, in her oilskin mack-intosh. She had been breathless, she had been a bad colour. I had thought it was the storm. Perhaps if I'd made some sort of enquiry . . . oh, what was the use of hindsight, it was no good going back over it all. The telephone shrilled at my elbow, and I snatched the receiver up, Aunt Meg's voice came strongly into my ear:

'Thea, I've just heard about Helen.'

'Heavens, that was quick, how on earth?'

'I was at the hotel with Ann, when Ruth phoned through. Now, listen, Thea, I'm going along to collect the twins from school. I'll take them home to The Moorings with me, till we know what James wants done. Ann's going straight to the hospital, naturally. Let James know what's happening, please.' Her phone went down, the line went dead, and I turned round in my chair to see James coming into my room.

'Will you sign the letters for me, please?' His face had a ravaged look. 'I'm going back to ICU.' He turned round to go out. Quickly I intercepted him, standing in front of him.

'My aunt has just rung,' I told him quickly. 'She's meeting the twins out of school. It seems she was with *your* aunt when Sister rang the hotel. She's taking the boys back with her to The Moorings. Miss Fellowes is coming on here.'

'Oh, I see, yes.' He shook his head, as though straining to gather his thoughts. 'Believe it or not, I'd forgotten the boys,' his smile didn't quite come off. 'It's very good of Lady Westering. I'll fetch them as soon as I can.'

'James . . . Mr Mayling, please don't hurry. Aunt Meg won't expect you to.' I wanted to say far more than that, but the words seemed to stick in my throat. And, anyway, he was going across to Ruth.

Her door had a long, frosted glass panel, and as it closed to behind him, I saw her small form meet his large one, saw them merge and unite. He had everything to thank Ruth for. She had saved his mother's life. She would comfort him too, for that's what fiancées were for.

I wish I could have done more, I thought, dragging my eyes away from the single blurred outline that was James and Ruth combined. I shut the door, *my* door, that didn't boast a glass panel. I applied myself to signing the letters, and clearing up the office. I left the hospital just after five p.m.

By then the storm and rain had ceased, but everywhere was soaked. I drove swiftly along the coast road, avoiding the miniature lakes which flowed at the sides where the overworked drains were blocked. Even the drive of The Moorings was puddly, and the smell of pine was strong from the hedge of cupressus which boundaried the property off.

William and Barry were in the kitchen, demolishing bread and butter, looking solemn and anxious, or William was; Barty was asking for cake. Aunt Meg cut him a generous slice, and ate a piece herself, absent-mindedly looking over at me. 'I'm going to suggest they stay here, Thea, till Helen can cope again. I don't see how her sister can have them, not with the hotel to run.'

'Have them stay *here*!' I stared at her.

'Yes, why not?' she said. She frowned slightly, and drew me away. I remembered to lower my voice.

'Aunt Meg,' I hissed, 'do you realise it might be for several weeks? Even when Helen comes out of hospital, she'll be on partial bed-rest. She won't be able to look after the children, and no one can be sure when James will be able to get suitable outside help.'

'I want to have them, I shall love it,' she said, 'and

John will agree with me. We've got plenty of room, and I've got the time, all the time in the world.' She returned to the table, poured milk for William, added a drip of tea. 'And there's the dog too, he'll have to come.'

'His name's Badger,' Barty supplied.

'Is Nan going to die?' William asked, looking straight at me. His eyes were huge behind his glasses, his question shook us all, even the seemingly uncaring Barty, who burst into noisy tears, and rushed to Aunt Meg, hiding his face in her knees.

'Of course Nan won't die,' I said, mentally crossing my fingers. 'She's staying in hospital to get well again, but it may take a week or two. You'll be able to go and see her soon, when she's feeling a little better.'

'I want to have a word with my father,' William sounded very grown-up, but his voice was trembling, so was his lip, and his face was turning red.

'Of course you do, William,' Aunt Meg said quickly (just in the nick of time) 'and Daddy will tell you everything when he comes in.'

'Does he know we're here?' William's face calmed, and he drank his milky tea from the blue china mug with the Princess of Wales on the side.

'Yes, he knows. I told him myself,' I replied, whilst my thoughts did a skid. What would James have to say to Aunt Meg's plan to board the boys, to look after them, for several weeks, perhaps? He would never agree, I was quite sure. On the other hand, he might. The Moorings wasn't far from Northbarn—merely the length of the village. He would be able to see them far more often than if they were at the hotel, which was a good mile on the other side of town.

'I still think it's too big an undertaking,' I repeated to

Aunt Meg, when the boys had gone into the garden to give the tortoise her tea.

'I love children, I don't see it that way.' She wiped up a blob of jam.

'I don't want to sound like a nag,' I persisted, 'but they're boisterous, healthy young boys. You're nearly seventy, and all right, I know . . . I *know* you don't feel, nor look it. But all the same, it's too much to take on.'

'Here comes John,' she said abruptly, looking out of the kitchen door at the big white Lancia nosing up the drive. It was closely followed by a black Rover, James' car, of course. Both men came into the house, but after the briefest of greetings, I went out into the garden to join the boys. James and Aunt Meg needed to talk, Uncle would arbitrate. I wouldn't be needed, and I mustn't interfere.

The twins were having the time of their lives throwing pebbles over the fence, down on to the Undercliff Walk, some eighty feet below. They seemed unmoved by the fact that walkers might be down there. I got the feeling that they rather hoped they were. I had never had much to do with children. Perhaps now's the time to learn, I thought as I watched them giggling together and butting each other like goats. The tortoise had declined to eat her lettuce, they had overwhelmed her too; she was huddled back, deep inside her shell.

After what seemed a very long time, James appeared on the terrace steps. The children raced towards him, with ecstatic cries of, 'Dad!' They crashed against him, two small figures in scarlet anoraks, two blobs of colour against his dark grey suit. He brought them over to where I stood, they were clinging to his hands, dragging on them, skidding their feet in the grass: 'Lady

Westering's just made me a gallant offer,' he said, trying to jest.

'I heard about it,' I smiled at him.

He looked down at the boys: 'And you're lucky lads,' he told them. 'Aunt Meg Westering wants you to stay here with her for a little holiday. You'll like that, won't you? You know you've always said how much you'd like to live in the house on the cliff.'

'Are you coming too?' Barty asked, and William echoed his words.

'No, but I'll see you most days, and when Nan's a little better you'll be able to go and see her in hospital.'

They both nodded, but both looked doubtful: 'Will we have to go to school?' Barty enquired, and Aunt Meg, shaking blankets out on the terrace, told them, in firm but kindly tones, that they would.

'She's in her element,' I said to James, as I climbed into his car. I was going with him to Northbarn to help pack the children's things, and a case for Helen Mayling in hospital. His car was sumptuous, I sank back in it, as it purred between the hedges and nosed down the rough cliff lane to the village street.

'It's an undertaking on her part,' he said, unknowingly using my words, and also expressing what I really felt inside. 'It's an undertaking on her part and an imposition on mine.' He said this in a tight-lipped fashion, he didn't look happy about it. He was the kind of man who I felt quite sure would hate accepting favours. He was doing so for the twins' sake, but I could see it hadn't been easy, not at all easy for him to say 'yes' to Aunt Meg. What would make things even more difficult for him (and I could have been wrong about this) was that I felt he didn't always get on with Uncle John. If this was the case, I could understand it for, goodhearted though Uncle was, he was also inclined to override, to think he knew best about most things, and to say 'pooh' to other people's ideas. So, poor man, I thought, he was in a cleft stick, he had got to accept help now for the interim period until he had sorted things out. Perhaps he would bring his marriage date forward, if Ruth was agreeable. A month would be all the notice Ruth would need to give to St Stephen's. Aunt Meg would have the boys for a month, I was sure.

It took less than five minutes to reach Northbarn, turn the car up its short, straight drive. Its thatch looked dark from the recent storm, its grey walls pearly pale. A swathe of purple clematis added dramatic colour, the lilacs drooped and gave off a musky scent. 'What a lovely garden,' I remarked, but caught my breath at the sight of a pointed white face at one of the windows, as we walked across the lawn. It disappeared with a kind of flick, James smiled as he got out his key:

'That'll be Badger jumping off his look-out post on the sill, and rushing across the hall to greet us,' he said. He opened the door, and motioned me in, and yes, there was Badger, dancing a mad sortie round our feet.

The hall was an almost perfect square, the stairs ran up at one side. A grandfather clock tocked in a corner, a copper bowl of roses (creamy white ones) sat on a table of oak. James got out cases and zipper-bags from a cupboard under the stairs. 'Let me help,' I said, taking two from him, and I followed him up to the bedrooms. The sun beamed through a westerly window, making patterns on his shoulders, lattice patterns, moving down to his heels. As for the house, it was charming, a country house of style. It was homely too, with a lived-in feel, it had a welcoming air. Houses may be inanimate objects, but most have atmosphere. I liked Northbarn's atmosphere, I felt happy people had lived there: still did, of course. We reached the top of the stairs.

'The boys' room is here,' he said, opening a door with a flourish. 'You'll find all their things in those drawers and cupboards.' He stood back to let me pass. 'I'll see to Mother's case myself. I know what she's likely to need.' He disappeared with the speed of light, and I knew that he was embarrassed. It *was* embarrassing, being closeted in his house together, like this. I ought to be Ruth, but Ruth was on duty, and would be till nine p.m. So, for heaven's sake, get on with it, I behested myself, opening the first of the cupboard doors. I packed enough clothes for a fortnight, I packed one or two toys as well. I was trying to make up my mind about books; the wall unit held a whole row of them, when James came in and looked over my shoulder.

'Better take a few,' he said. 'They love being read to at bedtime, a job my mother does. I like to take it on when I can, but those times aren't very often. A Registrar's work is never done, and the hospital's tentacles are long and strong, and easily reach as far as Pleydon village!'

'I'm sure they do, but don't worry,' I said, 'Aunt Meg will read to the boys, or I will; we'll see they don't miss out.' It was my turn to feel embarrassed, it must be catching, I thought. I hastily picked out *Bosun the Boatman* and *Robin's Magic Garden*, stuffed them in one of the cases and closed the lid.

James bent to fasten it down, as it lay on top of the bed. His back was to me, but I could see his face and front view in the mirror. As he straightened up, he saw me looking, our glances met in the mirror. He turned round and sat down on the bed: 'The children will make a great deal of work, and considerable inconvenience.'

'You mean at The Moorings?'

'I mean at The Moorings.'

'My aunt will enjoy every second.'

'But *you'll* be involved.'

'I expect I'll survive. I'll be out all day, anyway.' And I might have added a rider to this, something to the effect that the boys would keep us on our toes and provide some interesting moments, but the telephone started to ring in the hall, and it stopped conversation dead. It linked us in mutual alarm for a second, then James was out of the room, out and across the landing, thudding down the stairs, thoughts and hand already going out to the instrument on the table, next to the roses. I heard him snatch it up. And I stood in the bedroom doorway and listened, unashamedly listened. It was the hospital, I was quite sure, it had to be about Helen—about his mother—then I heard him say:

'Ruth? Yes, yes, I see . . . speak up.' And after that I closed the door, after all I couldn't eavesdrop, not when the caller happened to be Ruth. I heard the ting of the telephone bell as he put the receiver down, then his steps coming up the stairs; he was taking them two at a time. In he came, smiling, relaxed. 'That was Ruth,' he said, 'she's just been down to Intensive Care. Mother's asking about the boys. She even asked Ruth to give me a message about something in the oven, says to take it out, and switch the cooker off!'

We both laughed: 'I'm so glad,' I said, 'that can only be good news. I mean your mother . . .'

'Her brain's clear which, of course, is a very good sign.

She'll be in Intensive Care for about a week, I should think. After that it'll be the cardiac ward.'

'I'll see to the thing-in-the-oven, if you like,' I said as we went downstairs. So he took the cases out to the car whilst I went along to the kitchen, found oven gloves and opened the cooker door. On the middle shelf, rising domed from its tin, was a large fruit cake. I slid it out under Badger's appreciative nose.

'So that's what it was,' James said, as he came back in. 'Let's take it with us, shall we? It'll help your aunt out, perhaps.' We set it in a wicker basket, just as it was, in its tin. I waited for him to lead the way out, but he still stood there in the doorway.

'We can go,' I said, 'we've done everything. I've switched the cooker off. We're all set, all ready to go.'

'I think, not quite,' he said, 'unless you plan to go home in those,' he pointed to my hands, which still wore the padded oven gloves.

'Good heavens, sign of old age, like going out in one's socks!' I made to remove the gloves, but he did so for me, slipping them off as though I were a child. He kept one of my hands in his, I did nothing to pull it free:

'Thank you, Thea, for helping me,' his voice was low and gentle, and very moving, *so* moving that its effect was even greater than the warmth of his fingers curling hard round mine.

'Thanks aren't necessary.' I looked straight into his eyes—pale grey, tawny-flecked eyes, darkening to slate. I couldn't look away from them, they seemed to bind me to him. And I wanted him to kiss me so much I thought I would die of wanting. I thought of Ruth, just once, just fleetingly. I felt him pull me closer, then Badger barked, splitting my head . . . splitting the moment wide . . .

wide open . . . James's hand dropped to his side:

'We'd better go,' he looked angry, flushed.

'Yes, of course,' I said. I followed him across the hall, then the phone began to ring, to ring again with its loathsome din beside the bowl of roses. I resisted the urge to give it a violent poke.

He answered it whilst I stood on the front-door steps and drew in air—lungfuls of rain-sweet air that did nothing for me at all. Behind me I heard James saying: 'Yes, of course I'll tell her. Yes . . . yes . . . I understand. Yes, we're leaving now.' I turned round as he ended the call. Had it been someone for me? 'That was Lady Westering,' he said, slamming the front door shut. We began to walk across the lawn to the car: 'Your friend Hugh Delter is at The Moorings. He's there to call for you. It seems you have a theatre date, and your aunt points out that you're cutting it fine, have barely got time to change. Why on *earth* didn't you say so?' He looked even more furious.

'Aunt Meg flaps,' I said, climbing into the car. I had forgotten Hugh, forgotten our date, but in no way would I admit it. It would have made Hugh seem of no account, which certainly wasn't the case, nor was it fair; he deserved far better than that.

We set off down the short drive, Badger on my knees, the cake smelling like Christmas in the back. 'I'll roust up the Domestic Agency first thing tomorrow,' James said. 'I've had an advert in the local Gazette since the end of April. I can't understand the lack of response, not with all this unemployment. Northbarn House is hardly the back of beyond.' His brow was knitted, his mouth was set, he looked older than his years.

'It's a beautiful house, in a perfect setting, and it's got

a lovely atmosphere,' I said quickly, sounding placatory, but meaning every word.

'I'm glad you like it,' he snapped the reply.

But I fancied he relaxed, just a little, as we drove down the village street.

CHAPTER FIVE

'IT WAS good, wasn't it,' Hugh said, as we came out of the theatre and made our way into the snack bar that served suppers after the show.

'Super!' I smiled at him, hoping he hadn't noticed that my attention had wandered during the first half-hour. My thoughts had kept going back to James, and his mother, and the children, but especially to James and our hurried trip out to his house.

I had eaten nothing since one o'clock, and the plaice and fried potatoes that were put in front of us tasted marvellous. 'What a crazy girl to go so long without food,' Hugh said, 'all because Helen Mayling collapsed. That shouldn't have upset you. Being a nurse, that should be an everyday thing.'

'No,' I said, 'when you know the patient. That makes all the difference. And then there was the business of Aunt Meg taking the twins.'

'And you flaring off with James Mayling, and forgetting about our date.'

'Oh Hugh,' I broke a piece of roll, looking at him in dismay.

'Because you did forget, didn't you?' His light brown eyes were accusing. His head was turned to me as we sat side by side at the bar.

'I forgot just temporarily.'

'In the heat of the moment, perhaps?'

'Well, yes, something like that, but don't for one

moment think that I didn't want to come tonight. I wouldn't have missed it for anything. I'd been looking forward to it all the week.' The show we had just seen was *HMS Pinafore*. Aunt Meg had bought us the tickets as a surprise.

'That's all right then,' Hugh said, and the awkward moment passed. He could get uptight very easily and couldn't hide what he felt. We had been out together three times in all, and each time had been a success. He was good company, very amusing and, much to my relief, he hadn't been annoyed when I suggested that we 'went Dutch', for I'd felt that was fair, bearing everything in mind. He began to talk about the shop, and as the meal progressed, James Mayling and the happenings of the day slipped farther and farther backwards. I made them slip back. I concentrated on Hugh.

'You look ravishing in black, Thea,' he told me over our coffee which came in tall beakers with a swirl of cream on top.

'Thank you kindly!' I smiled at him. I liked the compliment, but took it with an outsize bucket of salt. Hugh had made a survey of the bar the moment we entered it. He had quickly spotted the female 'talent', and this was habitual with him. He could no more help appraising women than I could help breathing; I just thanked heaven I wasn't in love with him. This didn't mean, however, that I wasn't fond of him. I was attached to him by old links; he had charm of a special kind— a kind of controlled recklessness that had its own fascination. He was fun to be with, and we all need fun at times.

'Black suits you, oddly enough, even with raven hair. It makes you look slightly wicked, in a genteel kind of way.' He turned his stool and one of his knees nudged mine.

My dress was black taffeta, with a full-gathered skirt, and a round neckline, not especially low-cut. It was the only evening-type dress I had with me, so I'd had to wear it tonight. With it I wore my hair piled high on top. James had seen me go off with Hugh. He and Uncle John had been having drinks in the hall when we'd left the house. Had *he* thought I looked ravishing? Somehow I doubted it. His glance had been less than cursory. He had other things on his mind, important things, and he didn't gawp like Hugh.

'Have you ever been in love, Hugh?' I asked as he turned his head to take in the charms of a young blonde girl making her way to the doors.

'I could love you easily,' his attention came back to me, 'if you allowed me to, that is, but that's against your rules.'

'I'm talking of love, not making love.'

'I thought they were the same.'

'Not always, as you know quite well.'

'Point taken,' he said. And he said it unsmilingly, covering my hand, as it lay on the counter top: 'Little Thea grown-up, interesting and remote, giving me no leeway at all, treating me with contempt.'

'We agreed.'

'Oh, we agreed,' he said. 'And we never break agreements! Come on, let's go, if you've finished, that is.'

I hadn't, but I drained my cup. I followed him out. The back of his neck looked a little belligerent.

On the way home—his car was a sports, pale blue and low-slung—I asked him what he thought of Aunt Meg's decision to board the twins.

'Provided she doesn't expect you to run around after them, I can't see a thing against it,' he said. 'It'll probably do her good. I know she's getting on a bit, but she's got the strength of an ox. She'll probably live to a hundred and get a telegram from the Queen.'

'I hope she does!' I looked at him sharply; his tone had been very odd.

'Well, so do I, naturally,' I saw him smile in the dark. 'And as to James Mayling, I expect he'll decide to bring his marriage date forward. Then he'll take his sons and the nubile Ruth back to Northbarn House, and that will be that, the problem will be solved.'

'I expect you're right.' The words he spoke drew pictures in my mind. It was extraordinary how vivid they were, vivid and painful . . . physically painful. I leaned forward over my knees.

'Of course, you and I could always get married, then you'd be upsides with Ruth!'

'Not a good enough reason.'

'No, maybe it's not.' He was laughing, and I joined in but I wasn't all that amused.

'You should watch points,' I told him, drawing my shawl round tight. 'One day you'll make a similar remark to some designing female, and get taken up on it, good and sharp.'

'I'll bear that in mind and play safe,' he said, as we passed a long van, a huge pantechnicon roaring its way to the port to catch the ferry. Its headlamps drenched the car with light.

And the lights were on at The Moorings as well, in two of the downstairs windows. Hugh nodded towards them, as he stopped on the gravel sweep: 'Looks as though they're waiting up.'

'Aren't you coming?' I opened the passenger door, but he snapped it to again.

'No, I'll say goodnight to you here, so far as you'll permit. I can't stand Meg's prating tonight.' He turned my face to his: 'Goodnight then, Wicked Lady . . . would that you were,' he sighed. I felt the pressure and smooth of his lips, the rough graze of the moustache. Since that first Sunday on the beach he had never attempted force. He didn't now. Yet I angered him, I felt the anger in him. Sometimes I wondered why he kept asking me out. 'Till Saturday then,' he called, as I mounted the steps to the house, 'I'll give you a ring, to arrange a time.'

Aunt Meg was in the sitting-room in a droopy nightie and cardigan, a glass of whisky tilting in her hand: 'Do you want a nightcap?' she asked me.

'No, not a thing,' I said. 'It was a super show. I'm so glad you managed to get tickets.'

'Did Hugh enjoy it?'

'As much as me. He loves Gilbert and Sullivan. There's no fresh news about Helen, I suppose?'

'No, nothing, at least, nothing fresh. I rang a short time ago.' She took a gulp of her drink.

'The next ten days are bound to be worrying, and the next three weeks will be tricky. With care I'm sure she'll recover, though, but she'll have to re-order her life. Two little boys to look after are too much.'

'Yes, I know. James blames himself. I feel very sorry for him.'

'Did the children settle off all right?'

'He stayed until they did. I've put them in the second guest-room, the one with the twin beds. I told James not to hurry about getting domestic help. If necessary I can

have the boys until he and Ruth get married. I'm fond of
Helen. I want to help her. What happened today really
shook me. By helping James I'm helping her, because
then she won't worry about him, nor about the children.
She'll know they're in safe hands.'

'The safest hands this side of the Wash,' I said, going
over to kiss her. Soon after that we went upstairs,
moving quietly, for as well as Uncle John who needed his
full quota of sleep, there were two little boys in the
guest-room opposite mine. Aunt Meg had left them a
nightlight: 'Just in case,' she said, 'I don't want them to
wake up frightened, and wonder where they are.'

She went in to see them, I didn't, I entered my own
room. But even in there things were different, for on the
end of my bed was a round, curled-up blob of dog, very
gently snoring . . . Badger Mayling, making himself at
home. 'Now who said you could sleep here?' He rolled
over on to his back, showing his keel, wanting his
tummie rubbed. There was no sign of his basket, which I
supposed must be downstairs. He must have streaked up
when no one was looking. 'But why *my* bed?' I asked
him, knowing I'd let him stay. He stayed every night
after that. Aunt Meg tutted a bit, but didn't stop him.
Hugh said, 'Lucky dog!'

Helen Mayling progressed steadily, and had no serious setbacks. After a week in Intensive Care she was
transferred to the cardiac ward. After two weeks in
there, she went to her sister Ann Fellowes at the hotel.
James engaged a trained nurse to look after her.

'He's taking no chances. I admire him for it,' Aunt
Meg said. She had been to see Helen, and taken the
children, but they hadn't stayed very long. 'She's looking forward to moving back into her own house soon. At

least she's resigned to the fact that she can't look after the twins; although she insists that *they* didn't worry her.'

They had settled down well at The Moorings, but we'd had it easy so far. They were at school all day during the week, and James came most evenings, whenever he was free, to get them ready for bed. It was high summer now, of course, so there were riotous games in the garden. I joined in sometimes, when I wasn't out with Hugh. At weekends James took them home to Northbarn, so they had the best of both worlds. No doubt he and Ruth took them out on treats. Occasionally, when James was on duty, I gave them their tea and bath. I enjoyed their bedtime, they were less rowdy then; they were pliable little boys, asking for stories which I made up out of my head. Perhaps I'd inherited a modicum of talent from one, or both, of my parents, for those stories fairly flowed out of me; the boys' rapt faces inspired me, so did their cries of: 'Ooh, that's smashing, Thea!'

'James is still splitting himself trying to find a house-keeper,' Ruth remarked, one day in the office, after James had gone. 'He's seen half a dozen 'hopefuls', but he didn't like any. He's hard to please.' She seemed to be rather amused. 'He's dying to be independent of your aunt and uncle, you know, but he won't risk his children, not even to achieve that.'

'I admire him for it. I call that unselfish,' I replied with considerable heat. Ruth stared back at me in surprise. I wished she would go away and let me get on with my work. James, without any explanation, had abandoned the system of tapes. We were back to the old dictation methods, with all their previous hazards. I liked it better, liked the personal contact, but there are two sides to most things; the flip side to this one was struggling with outlines again.

'The trouble will be,' Ruth seated herself, unclipping her petersham belt, 'when the boys break up from school in two weeks' time. James can't very well take any leave, not when we're minus a houseman. It's all systems go till the Board get their finger out.'

'Oh dear, yes, I suppose so.'

'And talking of leave,' she went on, 'I'm taking mine on Friday week, returning ten days later. I'm not going far, only into Kent. My father's a GP there.'

'Who will be in charge here?' I was making a note of the dates.

'Staff Nurse Cater. There shouldn't be problems. I'm not indispensable.' There was a very slight edge to her voice, and glancing swiftly at her, I couldn't help thinking that she looked due for some leave. A ward sister's load was a heavy one, and Lytton Ward was full. Vinton Ward was much the same, so Miss Reenham told me. We still ran into each other at lunchtime most days.

On the day before Ruth was on leave, Mr Tell made his way to my room. He was off skull traction, and was wearing a cervical collar. He was allowed to be up for most of the day, and he tried to make himself useful— help the nurses at mealtimes, and raise other patients' morale. His only fault was his mania for making tours of the Unit. He was bored and he liked to see what was going on. My door was wide open and he walked straight in, his high, stiff collar giving a look of hauteur to his nice blunt features, making him seem to be looking down his nose. He was wearing pyjamas, no dressing-gown—we were in a heat-wave period—he sat down on one of the vinyl chairs. He came straight to the point, with devastating swiftness, before I could turn him out, and remind him that the office was out of bounds:

'I believe your aunt wants a housekeeper. My wife's mentioned it. She says there's some question of two little lads, that she wants some living-in help. My sister Angela wants the job. She's just come back from Australia, she's been looking after a family of five out in Canberra. My wife thought . . .'

'Mr Tell, it's not my aunt who's needing help, it's Mr Mayling.' I managed at last to stop him in his flow. He looked at me, over his collar, in start surprise:

'Mr Mayling? *Our* Mr Mayling, you mean, Mayling the surgeon?'

'Yes,' and 'yes' was as far as I got, for James was in the doorway. He had come to sign his letters. His gaze went to Mr Tell:

'Shouldn't you be in the ward,' he began; but Mr Tell cut him off short:

'Miss Westering says you want a housekeeper, sir. She was telling me about it. I happen to know of someone, my sister, Angela.'

'Perhaps,' James smiled woodenly, 'we could talk about it later.' He held the door even wider: 'You're trespassing in here.' He smiled again and touched Mr Tell gently on the shoulder. He would never upset a patient; his touch took the sting from his words. Mr Tell went out. James came in and shut the door.

But there was no kindly touch for me, and his look was withering. It was quite obvious what he thought. He thought I'd been interfering, trying to fix his domestic arrangements, and get rid of the boys. He began to sign his letters without a single word. I couldn't stand it. I had to try to explain:

'It wasn't as it seemed when you came in,' I began, 'I wasn't discussing you with him, it wasn't like that at all. He came straight in here and began to tell me all about his sister. He thought it was my aunt who needed housekeeping help. Naturally, I told him it was you.'

'He shouldn't have been *in* here, should he?' he kept on signing. 'You should have turned him out, used firmness and tact.'

'Yes, I know I should.'

'Of course you want to help Lady Westering *and* yourself, perhaps?' He looked at me and a question hung in his eyes. I answered it, for I knew what it was. I was glad of the opportunity to tell him how I felt about the boys:

'When Barty and William eventually go, I shall miss them,' I said. 'We all get on very well together, and the last thing I'm trying to do is to pull strings to manoeuvre your children out.'

'Nevertheless, I ought not to let any oppportunity slip,' he said thoughtfully, but he smiled as well, and I knew I had struck the right note. But what I had said was perfectly true, I *was* getting fond of the boys, they were growing on me, perhaps because they were his.

The last letter was read and signed. He passed the folder to me, then looked through the viewing window into the ward: 'I might as well go in and see Tell,' he said, 'something may come of it. Valerie, my late wife, thought a lot of Angela Tell. She used to baby-sit for us, before she emigrated. I'm talking, now, of five, nearly six years ago. Angela Tell was reliable, likeable as well. I wonder if she's here for good, or just wants a job for a time? I'll go and see Tell, I'll go and do it now.'

He went off with a swish and a flourish, I could tell he

was excited. I watched him cross the ward and open the door of the day room, I hoped that things would turn out as he wished.

They did, and within three days, starting from Sunday morning, Angela Tell was installed at Northbarn House. I saw her when she came to The Moorings, with James, to fetch the children. Aunt Meg had known her before she emigrated, and was pleased to see her again. She was a brown-faced, rather lined-looking woman in her fifties. Her hair was a faded russet and looked as parched as her skin, but her smile was wide and her eyes were kind; they lit when she saw the boys: 'I knew you two when you were babies. I expect we'll get along fine.' They shook hands, and Badger wagged his tail.

'Is she in England for good?' I asked, as the car drew off, William and Barty waving from the back.

'Oh yes, dear, she's not going back, that's why she can take a job. But I can't see her staying at Northbarn, not once James is married. Of course Ruth may have decided to carry on working for a time. All James said was that he and Angela have agreed on a three-months' trial. If, at the end of that time either party want to break, they can, with no hard feelings on either side.'

'How typical of James to dot all the "i"s and cross every visible "t",' I said waspishly, and sounding exactly, but exactly like Miss Reenham. I had better watch out, or in thirty years' time I might be a second edition. Feeling depressed I went in to make my bed.

Susan turned out to be a very able Acting Sister. She was every bit as strict as Ruth with the nursing team and auxiliaries, but she was less secretive, she was more open and a great deal noisier. One heard her coming long before she arrived.

We had four new admissions, three of them hip replacements, one of them an accident case—a student from the University. He was badly smashed up and for several days his life hung in the balance. By the sixth day he was out of danger, but was still on a drip (an intravenous infusion to maintain his body fluid). He was on four-hourly observations—pulse, respiration and blood pressure; he was a heavy case, and the ward was under-staffed. I would so much have liked to help, if only to do his obs., but I knew it was no good asking, hands would be thrown up in horror. The only thing I could do for him was read out his get-well cards; he had dozens of them from fellow students and friends. 'Most of the mail in this ward seems to be for Paul,' Susan said. She was quite right. We hung his cards over his bed.

Over lunch one day with Miss Reenham—who kept me abreast of all news—she told me that she had been invited to Eileen Frewin's wedding. 'It's a Register Office affair,' she said, 'I expect I shall go. You'll be gone by then, won't you?'

'Yes,' I said, 'I shall.' The date of Eileen's wedding was September the twenty-fourth. I would be in Town then, doing my job, my proper rightful job; my clerical job at St Stephens' would be at an end. 'It'll be lovely to be nursing again,' I emphasised to Miss Reenham.

'Everyone to their trade,' she said, 'or should I say "profession". I expect they'll soon be advertising for a girl to take your place. Perhaps she'll work with you for a time.'

'I doubt that,' I replied. 'There's not much I could teach her, I've only just learned it myself . . . very sketchily,' I added under my breath.

The next wedding, of course, will be the Mayling-

Filey one: '*If* it ever comes to fruition,' Miss Reenham pursed her mouth.

'Why do you say that?' I asked quickly, and of course I knew I shouldn't. She was gossipping and I ought to have closed my ears.

'Well, she's gone off on leave on her own, looking decidedly strained.'

'Mr Mayling's busy, he couldn't get off.'

She gave me a pitying look: 'Where there's a will, there's a way,' she said, skimming the skin off her coffee. 'Anyway,' she put her spoon down and flashed me a brilliant smile, 'we shall see, won't we, but my hunches are usually right.'

The rest period had started when I got back to the Unit. The ward was quiet, most patients were dozing before their visitors came. Jane Planner, the second-year nurse, was writing at the ward desk. Susan wasn't back from lunch, but Junior Staff Nurse Kerne was checking the drugs just up from Pharmacy. I could see Mr Tell in a chair by his bed, reading a paperback. He was holding it high to accommodate his neck. I went on the ward to tell him about his out-patients' appointments; he was due to be discharged next day at noon.

On my way out I glanced at Paul Merrick. I nearly always did. His bed was just inside the doors, he was sleeping, his head thrown back. He looked young and somehow defenceless, I stopped and looked down at him. His left arm was in plaster, the other one was splinted to hold the drip needle steady in his vein. It was then that I saw—more by luck than judgment, or perhaps it was my training—that his drip had ceased, there was interruption of flow. I should have called a nurse, of course I should, but I didn't think of that. I simply acted, and acted fast, moving close to his bed. My eye went to the infusion bottle at the top of apparatus. It was two-thirds full, no trouble there. I inspected the giving-set, no kinking, no blockage, no obvious cause. It had to be venous spasm. And still I didn't call a nurse, I had re-started drips before, and would again, and would now; I began to stroke Paul's arm, along the vein, above the injection site. I stroked gently, but firmly too, taking care not to jolt the needle. He stirred and woke, I reassured him, just as the drip re-started, re-started evenly, rhythmically, drop by lovely drop, twenty-five drops per minute, I counted every one. 'You can go back to sleep now,' I said. I'd tell Susan about this, of course, just in case the vein should spasm again.

It was then, as I made to turn away, that I realised I wasn't alone. At the foot of the bed stood James Mayling, and a scared-looking Learner Nurse Kyle. James' face wore a stunned expression, but behind it anger lurked. I knew it did. I could recognise the signs.

'Go into the office and wait for me there,' his voice was stiff and terse. He drew the curtains round Paul's bed. I turned and went out of the ward.

In the office I stood by the window and tried to quell my nerves. There would be trouble in plenty, I knew that, I had no right to touch a patient. Paul had been perfectly safe with me, I had simply risked my own neck. I had stepped out of line. I wasn't a staff nurse here. I tried to rehearse what I'd say to James when he came storming in. But surely he would see I had acted instinctively, out of knowledge and training. He would *have* to understand. He was coming, I could hear him. He opened the door, shut it, stood by the desk. His face was granite, his eyes were steel. I felt stifled and couldn't breathe, daren't breathe, the back of my legs went weak:

'Why didn't you summon Staff Nurse Kerne to attend to Paul Merrick?' His question was snapped out, was straight to the point, it floored me at the start.

'I . . . don't know,' I heard myself stutter.

'You'll have to do better than that.'

'Well then, I just didn't think about it,' I burst out in a rush, 'I saw his drip had stopped and I took steps to get it started—correct steps. I did the same as I would have done at St Mildred's.'

For some reason this seemed to inflame him, he leaned forward over the desk. 'But you're not at St Mildred's, are you? You're here, and *not* as a nurse. You're here as a clerical worker, you're *non*-nursing staff. You had no right to attend a patient in a nursing capacity. Your job is in here . . . in this office.' He banged his fist down on the desk.

'It still doesn't alter the fact that I'm a qualified nurse!' I choked.

He came round the desk to me, straight and ramrod stiff: 'I don't care if you're Florence Nightingale reincarnated!' he blazed. 'Whilst you're here you'll do the job that Sir John put you in for, the job you came for, and limit yourself to that! If you can't be trusted to steer clear of the patients, you'd better keep out of the ward.'

I stared at him, I stared at the floor. His words had a cutting effect. If someone else had said them I wouldn't have minded so much. I might have been upset and frustrated, but I wouldn't have felt so . . . knifed. His words hurt. I turned my back on him.

I was struggling with tears, and he must have known it. Silence fell on the room. Out of it he began to talk, but much more quietly: 'You see,' he said, 'hospital ethics need to be observed. When they're not . . . well, the balloon goes up. Imagine the fuss there'd have been if the principal nursing officer had come in and seen you, had caught you setting young Paul's drip to rights. There'd have been trouble for the nurse in charge—for Staff Nurse Cater.'

'Susan was still at lunch.'

'But she'd have been held responsible, in Ruth's absence. You know that perfectly well.'

His mention of Ruth put stiffening in me. I was able to face him again: 'Yes, I know it.'

'Then why not conform, it's not for very much longer.'

'You're right, it's not for much longer,' I wanted to hit back now. 'In a little over five weeks I'll be back in my proper job, nursing again, caring for people, not watching others do it.'

'And thinking you could do it better?'

'In some instances, yes.'

'I think you could too. I have a feeling you're a very good nurse indeed.'

I looked at him hard. Did he mean it, or was he sending me up, or being kind, or pouring a little oil? He moved closer to me: 'Oh, I mean it,' he smiled, resting his hands on my shoulders, 'and off the record, and just between the two of us, Thea, I think you did a splendid job for Paul.'

'Thank you,' was all I could manage. His words took my breath away. It was such a complete volte-face—so typical of the man.

'I didn't intend to upset you.'

'You didn't,' I averted my eyes from his, partly because of the lie, but mostly because I wasn't sure what might show in mine, so I kept on looking down at the

floor. Our feet were close, almost touching, he wore
black slip-on shoes; his hands were warm, I could feel
their warmth through my white overall coat. They were
moving, cupping my shoulders, tightening, drawing me
up to him, I felt the brush of his lips against my hair.

'Pity you can't nurse here.' He was being brisk again,
setting me free, moving back, looking unconcerned and
unmoved . . . yes, unmoved. How could he not feel
something, when I felt so much? I watched him make for
the door: 'I've an out-patients' clinic at two, mustn't
keep my public waiting!'

I agreed that he mustn't, I went through the motions, I
closed the door after him. Then, even whilst I railed at
myself for being so weak and mawkish, I stood by my
street window and looked down to where he'd emerge
from the tower building and cross to the out-patients'
block. And presently, out he came, not looking all that
much smaller, nor less disturbing, not even from four
floors up.

CHAPTER SIX

SUSAN WAS seeing relatives of patients up until four o'clock, but very soon after she came in to me, a cup of tea in each hand: 'I thought I'd have mine in here with you,' she kicked the door to with her heel, put the cups on the desk and sat down opposite me: 'I heard all about the little matter of Paul Merrick's drip.'

'I asked Nurse Kyle to report it to you.'

'She did, with embellishments! I suppose you got a rocket from Mayling?'

'He hit the roof,' I said, 'but calmed down afterwards,' I felt my face going red.

'You're dying to get back to nursing, aren't you?' She looked at me over her cup.

'To be honest, yes. I don't find anything else fulfilling enough. But thanks for not going on about me interfering, Sue. I had no business touching Paul's drip. James . . . Mr Mayling was right.'

'Never mind, I'm not Ruth. She'd have strung you up on a rope! Not that I'm talking against her, mind; she's a very decent sort. She's back on Wednesday,' Susan's face sobered, 'then my spell of power will be finished. Acting Ward Sister Cater will plummet to staff nurse again.'

'You've enjoyed it, haven't you?'

'To be honest, yes. And what is more,' she went on, 'I intend to apply for her job when she marries and leaves St Stephen's.' Her chin came out a little defiantly.

'I don't blame you one bit. I hope you get it.'

'I think I stand a chance. I'm twenty-seven, and I've held a staff nurse post for six years now. My husband and I don't want a family, we're both career-minded. I don't want to leave St Stephen's, so must grab my chances here. Ward sisters don't leave that often, most stay until they retire. Ruth Filey's an exception to the rule.'

'I hope you get it, I really do.' The tea tasted bitter. Susan would apply as soon as she knew when James and Ruth were marrying. I swallowed hard, listening to her words.

'I wish I knew when she was going. I like Ruth, but she's close. They *must* have made their plans by now.' She looked at me, biting her lip, 'Thea, I know I'm quizzing, and shoot me down if you like, but has your uncle, has Sir John said anything about it? I wondered if Mayling had mentioned the matter to him.'

I shook my head: 'Not so far as I know. I've not heard so much as a whisper.'

'Then I'll have to bide my time in patience, which doesn't come easy to me. Still, it's no good worrying.' She heaved an enormous sigh, then changed the subject and talked about the weekend: 'It's my Saturday off. I'm hoping to buy a dress for the barbecue.'

'And that,' I said, 'makes two of us, for I want to do the same.'

The barbecue to which Susan referred was being held at The Moorings on Thursday the twenty-ninth of July. Uncle John and Aunt Meg gave one every year, for the staff on the Ortho Unit, and for one or two surgeons from Wellbridge County too. Wives, girl-friends, husbands and boy-friends were also included. Each invitation card, sent out three weeks ago, had borne the words 'and partner' after the name. I could see, too, that The Moorings' garden would be perfect for a barbecue; for being so close to the sea, being part of the cliff itself, nothing ever grew in it, apart from hardy shrubs. There was, therefore, nothing at all to spoil, there was oceans of space, all that was needed was a dry and gale-free night. 'We open the terrace side of the house, and people spill in and out exactly as they want to,' Uncle John had said. 'We get a couple of waiters in, but do the cooking ourselves. It's splendid fun, you'll enjoy it, Thea, m'dear.'

'Perhaps we could meet tomorrow.' Susan broke into my thoughts, 'We could do our dress-hunting together, have tea at The Creamery afterwards. What do you say? It would make it more fun.' She looked at me, green eyes sparkling.

'Okay, you're on,' I said, smiling back, glad she had made the suggestion. I liked Susan, and I'm not very keen on buying clothes on my own. I like someone with me to lend an unbiased view.

And so it was that at three o'clock the following afternoon, we were in Hartington's department store, upstairs in the gowns sections, pushing evening and cocktail dresses round on the rails. We looked at dozens, but none was right. We grew more and more hot and fed-up. 'I wondered about a pants suit,' said Susan, 'something very lightweight. Last year several of the younger set came in knickerbockers, and jolly snazzy they looked too. Let's try that rail over there.' In the end she settled for a trouser suit in sunshine yellow cotton, but I still clung to the idea of a dress.

We hunted around in two more shops, all to no avail, and then, whilst on our way to the north end of the High

Street, we saw a dress on a model in the window of a
boutique. With one accord we stopped and looked at it.
It was the only dress in the window—a brilliant, striking
dress, scarlet silk, with a layered skirt, mid-calf length. It
had the new one-shoulder look and it was made for a tall
thin girl with black hair. The model was like myself:
'That's *your* dress!' Susan hooted.

'There's no price on it,' I demurred.

'You could try it on. What's the harm?'

'But supposing . . .'

She tugged my arm: 'Oh, come *on*, Thea! Have a bit of
courage . . . they want to sell it to someone. Why not
you, they might knock a pound or two off.'

They didn't, but I still bought it. I came out with it in a
box, a very up-market type of box, with little corded
handles, and the name 'Gabrielle' in copperplate on its
side. Never before, in the whole of my life, had I paid so
much for a dress. It was scary, yet gave me a kick as well.

'You couldn't not have bought it,' said Susan, 'it's
your dress absolutely. I'd like to see your Hugh's face
when you waft down the stairs in that. He's very charming, isn't he, terrifically good-looking?' She had met
Hugh, for she and Don (her commercial-artist husband)
had bought a clock from Geeson's the week before.

I agreed about Hugh's good looks, but my mind was
wandering; I was trying to work out whether my cheque
would bounce. I was still doing frantic sums in my head
when we got to The Creamery Tearooms, only to find
that the place was choc-a-bloc. 'It's no good, we'll have
to go to that new place on the front,' I said, turning to
push out again, but Susan caught hold of my arm.

'Cast your eye over there;' she said, with a tiny
movement of head. I did so, and saw what she had, or

rather, *whom* she had—James Mayling, with William and Barty busy with tall ice-creams, at a table for four, on the far side of the room.

'Is there no escape from him?' My heart turned over and over and over, like a hot drum in my chest.

'None. He wants us to join him, he's got a spare chair.'

'But there's two of us,' I protested weakly. Why did he have to be here? Why couldn't he stay at Northbarn and cut his grass? I followed Susan across the room, my long box impeding me. I got stuck between chair-legs, she turned to help me, and as we straightened up, we saw an additional chair being borne aloft to James's table by a stalwart lady with arms like rolling pins.

'He could get a camel to spit spring water in the middle of the Sahara!' Susan hissed out of the corner of her mouth.

'You've no excuse not to join me now,' he said, when we reached him at last; we stacked our parcels; the twins looked up and smiled. They were digging into their tall glasses, doing valiant work with their spoons. 'We came in here for those,' James said, nodding towards their ice-creams, 'but now that you've come . . . tea and cream cakes, please,' he said to the young waitress, 'and hang the rise in cholesterol level for once!'

'As the advert says, naughty, but nice!' Susan added pertly. She was easy with him, completely relaxed. I was neither, so talked to the twins. They told me how much they liked Miss Tell.

'She lets us call her Angela, she makes us chocolate fudge, and she reads to us at bedtime,' said Barty, clinking his spoon on his teeth.

'But she doesn't tell us fresh stories, she tells them out of a book. And you never finished the one about the

sailor with a sore foot,' William said, turning a reproachful glance at me.

'I like hearing about kangaroos and the cuckoo-billy
birds,' Barty put in, backing Angela.

'Kookaburras,' I corrected smiling, 'they're a kind of
laughing kingfisher.'

'Kookaburras, kookaburras,' they chanted, and
giggled together. It was plain they were happy. I was
glad for everyone's sake.

I started on a cream slice, and James drew me into the
talk between him and Susan; there was plenty to discuss.
There was Mrs Mayling (still doing well), the coming
barbecue, and last but not least, the clothes we had
bought, drawn attention to by Susan, indicating the
dress-box by my chair. 'Thea's broken the bank in the
hope of bringing her boy-friend up to scratch!' She was
only ribbing, and I managed to laugh, but I wished she
hadn't said it, not quite like that, not in front of James.

'Can I give either, or both of you a lift anywhere?' he
asked, half an hour later, when we stood on the pave-
ment outside.

'I'm meeting Don at the *Argus* office. I can manage to
totter that far,' Susan said, along with her thanks, 'and
Thea's got an assignation!'

'More an errand,' I said, 'I'm collecting a jug for Aunt
Meg from Geeson's, but it's only just round the corner,
so I can cope.'

'Then I'll leave you to your separate ploys.' His slow
smile came and went. Grasping a hand of each of the
boys, he hurried across the road. Susan went off in
another direction, whilst I turned into West Street,
which led into Park Street, which brought me to
Geeson's Antiques.

It was a small shop, exclusive, bow-fronted, it had a Dickensian air, like The Old Curiosity Shop, I thought, as I went inside. Mr Geeson and Hugh were engaged with customers, so I merely smiled from a distance, and walked round, looking at the stock. I had been to the shop several times, I found it fascinating, there was always something fresh to see, so the turnover must be good. The stock ranged from junk and bric-a-brac, to items of modest value, to selected small antiques of considerable worth. There were one or two pieces of furniture, like chairs and escritoires; there were odd-ments—a ship's barometer, an ancient-looking carriage lamp, and dozens of clocks, none of them keeping time. There were several ornaments on a wall unit, the ones low down caught my eye—three coloured-glass vases, I stooped to look at them. What, I wondered, gave an antiques collector his, or her, special thrill. Was it the beauty of the things they collected, or the fact that they were old, or their worth in pounds sterling, a kind of investment thing? I simply liked what took my eye, but today I mustn't be tempted, not after what I had paid out on my dress.

The customers were leaving. Hugh was showing them out. I turned to greet him, eagerly, quickly, forgetting where I stood, forgetting too that from my fingers dangled a long, hard box. I heard his shout: 'Take care! Watch out!' saw the look on his face at the same second as the box made contact, as my horrified ears heard a bump, and a fall, and a crash, and the shattering of glass. And hardly daring to turn, I saw the vases in fragments at my heels. The shelf was bare; well, of course, it was bare. Oh God, what had I done!

'Of all the clumsy, blundering idiots!' Hugh's flood of

angry words shocked me almost as much as what I'd done.

'I'm so sorry, Hugh! I'm so sorry, so sorry!'

'For Christ's sake, what were you doing, charging about in the shop with that!' he pointed to my box.

'I was clumsy, and I'm . . . just . . . very sorry!'

He was looking down at the glass, at the broken curves that still rocked from the fall, at the pointed dagger-like shards. He picked a piece up and looked at me, then dashed it down again. And his anger wasn't the blazing kind, it was cold and it went right through me. It felt like ice, it froze me where I stood.

'I'll pay, of course,' I said shakily, trying to move away. He didn't reply, I don't think he could, but Mr Geeson did. At some stage he had joined us, and brought a dustpan and brush:

'Now there's no need to worry, Miss Westering. Those vases were coloured glass, *just* coloured glass, worth five pounds each; we might even have sold them for three.'

'Well, thank goodness for that at least,' my laughter sounded thin. Hugh was bent double, clashing the glass in the pan.

'It was such a stupid thing to do,' his voice came up from the floor.

'But hardly a crime!' I snapped back, retaliating at last. He had been more than justly angry, even more than rude, he had been offensive, downright offensive, and I wasn't having that. 'Hardly a crime,' I repeated, as he rose.

He looked at me, his face was red, he was trying to rearrange it, not an easy task with his eyes still spitting hate. 'It was an accident, and I intend to pay,' I dived into my bag, found my wallet, put three five-pound notes on top of the dustpan of glass. Mr Geeson had gone, but over Hugh's shoulder I could see him at the counter, putting Aunt Meg's Toby jug into a box. 'I'll take the jug and get home,' I said, as Hugh went to speak to a customer. Mr Geeson showed me out, he came into the street with me, and stood at the kerb, solemnly shaking my hand:

'Don't worry about those vases, Miss Westering, don't give them another thought.' He was quaint, and courtly, and a little old-fashioned, his faded blue eyes were concerned.

'It's good of you to take it like that. I feel very badly about it,' I said, juggling my parcels, as he let go of my hand. 'I've left fifteen pounds with Hugh to pay for the damage, just in case he forgets to mention it.'

Now that, of course, was pure bitch, and hardly fair to Hugh. But bad feeling and insulting words are infectious, like chicken-pox. I made my way to the car park still feeling resentful and hurt. I wouldn't see Hugh for the next few days, he was off to Gloucestershire, to a country house sale that would take the best part of a week. I knew he was travelling tonight, overnight, and a good thing too, I thought, as I unlocked the car and slammed myself into it. Yet I found, as I drove through the crowded town, as I sped along the coast road, that my outraged feelings were moderating and I *could* see Hugh's point of view. The shop was very important to him, and I knew this only too well. It was things, rather than people, with him, he set great store by possessions. What a good thing I'd not smashed up a priceless antique.

I tried my dress on when I got home, at Aunt Meg's

request. Her approval was instant and unstinting: 'You look absolutely gorgeous, like a top-flight model straight off the cover of *Vogue*!'

It was high praise, but I knew she meant it. She always made me feel good. And I told her about the broken vases, but I played down Hugh's fury, I omitted to tell her the actual words he had said. 'Oh, for heaven's sake,' she exclaimed at once, 'let me pay for the damage, Thea. If it hadn't been for collecting my jug, you'd not have been at the shop.'

'It's all right, truly, Aunt Meg. I'd rather not,' I said.

She tutted a little, but didn't persist: 'You're as bad as your Uncle John!' She looked rather rueful as she said it, and I wondered what she meant. Then she gave me one of her twinkly smiles, and motioned me upstairs. 'Go and take your glad rags off, child, then come back here. There's something I want to explain to you, I should have done so before.'

'A nice or nasty something?' I asked, beginning to mount the stairs.

She laughed: 'I don't think it's either of those, more inevitable!'

When I rejoined her a few minutes later, she had two large sherries waiting. We took them out into the sunshine, and sat on the terrace wall. True to form, she got down to business at once. 'It's about my will.'

I sat up straight, nearly capsizing myself. 'Oh, Aunt Meg, what a grisly subject! Do we really have to?'

She nodded: 'Yes, we do, and now's the time to tell you, whilst I'm hale and hearty, and probably good for another twenty years.'

'Or even thirty.' I felt embarrassed; teasing her seemed to help.

'Or even thirty, but joking apart, one never knows,' she said. 'I won't go into boring details, I'll keep it as short as I can. But to go back a little in time, you know I was married before, before Uncle John; you know he's my second time round!'

'Yes, of course I know. Father told me. You married Uncle John roughly three years before I was born.'

'Twenty-five years ago. My first husband, Allan Drew, had died the year previously leaving me fairly well off, we'd had no children, I couldn't have them—a great grief to us both. I was forty-four when I married John, he was ten years younger. He has never, and never would, touch any of Allan's bequest. It was mine to do what I liked with, he said, but he wanted to be the provider, the sole provider of all the things relating to our marriage, to our life together, which of course I understood. In a will made on my remarriage, I left your uncle, with few exceptions, everything I possessed, which included the money from Allan, and he said nothing very much then. But last year—and it was Hugh's new venture that brought it up again—John suggested that I made a new will, leaving Allan's fund to my godchildren—namely you and Hugh, divided equally. Hugh has had part of his already, to buy the partnership. Yours is intact, and will come to you when I pass on! That's all!' She swigged the last of her drink. 'That wasn't so grisly, was it?'

'Oh, Aunt Meg!' I groped for words. I didn't know what to say. For what was the right thing to say when one was given news like that? 'It's good of you, kind and everything, but I don't want to think that far, not that far ahead, and it *is* grisly!'

She gave my knee a tap. 'We won't mention it again,

ever, but you mustn't be quite so fey. Making a will is hardly a death wish, it's a sensible business arrangement. For all my surface scattiness, I like things to be right, to be left in order.'

I said that I understood.

But death wish or no, I had dreams that night of a very unpleasant nature. The train accident, the scene in the shop, and Aunt Meg's talk of wills, bent and joined and twisted together to form the skeins of nightmare. Even when I awoke I still had a latent sensation of doom, a feeling that something appalling would happen to Aunt Meg, or to me, or to Hugh . . . and I wouldn't be able to stop it.

But I told myself I was being fanciful.

CHAPTER SEVEN

FIVE DAYS later, on the day of the barbecue, Hugh sent me flowers. They came to the hospital, cellophane-wrapped, with a little card attached: 'Sorry, please forgive me. All my love, Hugh.' The flowers were roses, a dozen dark red ones, I took them out of the wrapping, and sniffed each one; I was overcome with relief. I hate quarrelling, I loathe bad feeling, and the flowers seemed to indicate that Hugh felt the same. I decided to ring him up. The switchboard got the shop number for me, and a second or so later I was speaking to him, sitting at my desk. 'The flowers have come, they're gorgeous,' I said, 'thank you very much.'

'I'm glad you like them . . . that I did the right thing,' he sounded uncertain for once. 'I had them sent direct to the Unit, so that you got them early.'

'They're lovely,' I assured him. 'Did you do well at the sale?'

'Superbly well.' He told me about it, but I had to cut him off short, because Ruth came in, waving one of her lists. It was her first day back after leave, and I thought she looked a lot better—a better colour, she had even acquired a tan.

'I've just had word that Sir John and James, and the new houseman, Neil Pardon, are coming up to do a full round,' she said. 'They're bringing two medics as well. Here's the list for the notes.' It was very long, it would be a teaching round.

111

I dived into the cabinets, checking the notes with the list. I had met the houseman, Dr Pardon; he was newly qualified. He had done his six months on the medical wards, and was now on his surgical stint. His coming meant that James would be able to extend his out-patients' clinic, and do more in theatre, and have his weekends off. A good houseman was a great boon to consultants and registrars, for he made up the team, and took the strain from the load.

The little procession arrived on time, and went through on to the ward, Ruth and Uncle John leading, James and Neil Pardon behind, the two medical students at the rear. One of the students was Chinese and female, and doll-like in stature; her pigtail hung ruler-straight down the back of her coat. I saw James explaining something to her, she was looking up at him; then they all grouped round Paul Merrick's bed, and Ruth drew the screening curtains. I began my next job, which was filing X-ray reports.

An hour passed, the ward round ended, and Uncle and the students went off, leaving only James to bring the notes back to me. 'There's a new admission tomorrow,' he said. 'Daniel Barter for arthroplasty. You can make out the forms now, if you like—so far as you can, of course. I'll get his cards sent up from out-patients. I've no letters for you today. I shall swing a great deal of the paperwork on to Neil Pardon now. I think you'll find he'll use the dictating machine.'

'Oh, that'll be all right. I'll cope,' I said, digesting what he had said—the effect of it being that from now on I would hardly ever see him. Just as well, I told myself briskly, watching him go to the cabinets and open a drawer, and slam it shut again. He picked up my flowers, glanced at the card, and laid them down in a hurry

'Sorry, I thought they were meant for a patient.'

'No, they're personal.'

'Red roses for love!'

'So the saying goes.'

He halted in front of my desk. 'You haven't got long with us now, have you? The sands are running out.'

I didn't know whether to be pleased or regretful— neither, probably. 'I've a month to go,' I told him. 'I've no doubt it'll soon pass.'

'The post's being advertised in the *Gazette* this week.'

'I know. Uncle John told me that. I hope you get someone nice—I mean, someone efficient,' I added seeing his brows shoot up.

'I hope she'll be both. Eileen Frewin and you will be very hard to replace. And yes, I mean that. I seldom flatter, I'm not a fulsome type. Secretarial work might not be your forte, but you've coped with it very well.'

I blinked at him. I was so surprised that I nearly dropped down where I stood. I was just about to thank him, when Ruth came bustling in to ask me to ring the Occupational Therapy Department. 'Now that Paul Merrick's off his drip, and feeling better, but bored, I think we're going to have to try to alleviate his gloom. He likes doing jigsaws, he says, and I'm sure they've got some in Therapy. Ask them, Thea, we might as well do what we can.'

I agreed that we might. James went out. The hospital day wore on. I hoped to leave early, because of the barbecue. James came back at tea-time; he asked where Ruth was, I told him at tea; he decided to wait for her He stood by one of the filing cabinets, his elbow on the top, his nose a bare inch from Hugh's flowers, which

Nurse Kyle had put in a vase. James and red roses . . . I wished he had sent them. James and red roses, I thought. It would make a good title for one of Mother's books.

'It's good of your aunt to have the twins to stay overnight,' he said. 'It means such a lot to Angela Tell to come to the barbecue.'

'Well, you know Aunt Meg, any excuse to have the children round her, but this time there was a secondary reason, she thinks Angela Tell will be an authority on cooking out of doors.'

'Having come from Australia, you mean!' He laughed and so did I. 'She's a good indoor cook, I can thoroughly vouch for that. All I hope is . . .' But what he hoped I wasn't to learn just then, for Ruth returned and he slipped across to her room.

I hardly recognised The Moorings' garden when I turned up the drive that evening. There were tables and chairs and trestles, and trolleys being unloaded from vans; there were portable barbecues dotted about; there were iron grids and grilles, and metal trays, and bags of charcoal; there were lights being strung in the trees. The veranda and terrace was a welter of cutlery and crockery and paper cloths. People I had never seen before flashed in and out of the house, carrying and pushing, all under Aunt Meg's command. 'And don't forget the rosemary twigs for throwing on to the fires. It gives off such a delicious scent!' she instructed Uncle John. He had come home early, and was looking a trifle bemused.

We shall permeate the coastline from here to East-bourne, I thought, slipping into my scarlet dress, adding a red choker necklace, standing back to view myself full length.

'It's nice, Thea,' said a voice from the doorway, and in stepped Barty, closely followed by William, both of them ready for bed. 'We like red,' they said in unison.

I began to brush my hair. 'Don't you know you're supposed to knock before you come into a bedroom, especially a lady's bedroom, in a house that's not your own?'

'Have we got to go out again?'

'No, you can stay now you're here.'

'When will all the people be coming?' William stared out of the window at all the to-ing and fro-ing in the garden below.

'Not until eight o'clock. You'll both be fast asleep by then.'

'We won't be asleep if we keep awake.'

'Well, no, that's very true,' I laughed, and handed them over to Angela, who was in the guest-room opposite, folding their clothes and turning down their beds.

She and I went downstairs together to lend a hand in the kitchen which, like the garden, had been completely transformed. It was more like a food hall than a kitchen; there were edibles everywhere—skewered chickens, fork-tailed sausages, turkey wings, spare ribs, lamb chops, porterhouse steaks, cold lobster and prawns. There was brown and white bread, parsley and chive bread, brioche rolls and cheeses, bowls of salad, raspberries and cream, brandied peaches and melon, and enough drink to float the QE2.

Aunt Meg in a skirt like floral curtains was pouring barbecue sauce and basting oil into a row of jugs. Into each jug she flung a brush, and she gave us a short lesson on what to do once the food was wheeled outside. 'We don't need to start cooking for another half-hour,' she said, 'barbecued food tastes so much better if it's cooked and eaten at once.'

The fires had been lit by Uncle John, and the charcoal had stopped flaring and settled down into a steady glow. 'Exactly right,' he pronounced happily. The heat from them was intense, which wasn't unwelcome for the night was cool—not exactly cold, but not so close and warm as we would have liked.

An hour after that the garden, the patio and the terrace were streaming with guests. Everyone seemed to be in the party spirit; there was laughter, and chatting, and clinking, and sizzling too from the roasting meats, whilst the scent from the burning rosemary brought forth appreciative comments from every side. Most people sat down to eat, there were chairs enough, goodness knows. And how ever used to parties one is, it's not the easiest thing to gnaw one's way through a piping hot chop, or wedge of sirloin steak, and balance a glass, and manage to talk as well.

Hugh had come early to help with the cooking. I could see him wreathed in smoke—or was it steam?—turning sausages on the grid. Aunt Meg and I were looking out for any late arrivals; we welcomed several, including James and Ruth.

'Please forgive us, but we went to the hotel to see Helen first,' said Ruth. She admired my dress. Hers was green chiffon, drawn in with a sequined belt.

'Such a pity Helen couldn't come,' Aunt Meg smiled, 'but it would all have been too noisy and tiring. I do see that.'

'She's up to most things, but not parties yet,' James said quietly. He was immaculate in a light grey suit and a rather flamboyant tie. He had a thoughtful look about him, and Ruth did most of the talking as Aunt Meg led them over to the bar. I lost sight of them for some time after that, for Hugh and I were busy, cooking and serving as fast as we could go. The garden was crowded: I suppose, to be honest, it was just a shade overcrowded. I was glad to sit down at half-past ten and ease my feet out of my sandals. Hugh was still barbecuing steaks. From where I was sitting—half-way to the house—I could see James and Ruth. They were on the terrace with two other people, neither of whom I knew. Farther along, by the french doors, Miss Reenham was sipping coffee. She had her elderly mother with her—a timid little woman, who hardly spoke and who kept having sneezing fits. She was having one now, and I heard Miss Reenham admonish her quite severely: '*Blow* your nose. Mother . . . whatever will people think!' I knew they lived fairly near the hospital, opposite Ruth's flat. They had come in a taxi, but James was taking them home.

Music drifted from the sitting-room and hall. One or two couples were dancing. Aunt Meg had rolled the carpets back earlier on. I saw Hugh coming towards me, jerking down his sleeves. He pulled on his jacket, a black velvet one, gave me a cheerful grin. 'I think I've done my share of the chores, now I'm out to enjoy myself,' he said, pulling me up from the seat. 'Come on, let's go in and dance.'

'All right,' I buckled my sandals back on, and walked with him up to the terrace. We stopped to have a word with James and Ruth.

'It's a very good party,' James said, rising from his chair. I heard him ask Ruth if she wanted to dance, but she smiled and shook her head. She gave me the impression of having a great deal on her mind; she seemed to me to be preoccupied.

'She's doesn't exactly scintillate, does she, for all her physical charms,' Hugh said once we were out of range, and were flinging around in the hall to the pulsing beat of Adam and the Ants.

We changed partners several times. Hugh did the round of the nurses. He went down very well with them, they buzzed around him like flies. I didn't do so badly myself, and my knee stood up to the strain, for this must be the ultimate test, I thought, as Neil Pardon and I gyrated in a zig-zag over the floor. A colleague of Uncle John's (from Wellbridge) asked me to dance next. He was tall and so thin that when we danced I could visualise a skeleton, dry and bony, clanking inside his clothes. I suppose he would be around fifty, and as we talked together, I could see that despite his absence of brawn, he had undoubted charisma. He gripped my waist with a steely but flexible arm.

'He's too old for you,' Hugh said, when we met up again, 'but probably loaded, and I don't mean with excess flesh!'

He was a neuro-surgeon, I remembered suddenly, and brilliant in his field. I saw him claim Ruth for a dance, but when I looked round for James, I couldn't see him; he must have stayed outside. The dance was an 'oldie', a slow foxtrot, not Hugh's favourite kind, so we went off to get some coffee, and had just got our cups in our hands when Aunt Meg bore Hugh away to fix one of the tables. 'It keeps sagging, darling, and I fear for it,' she said. I finished my coffee with Eileen Frewin and Mr Martineau. They both looked very well and happy, Eileen in primrose linen, Robert in a light grey lounge suit, standing straight and tall, a stick (for safety) hanging over his arm.

The din in the house, once the guests started coming in from the garden, was raucous, and I wondered about the twins. They couldn't, I thought, be sleeping through it, they might even be alarmed. Slipping away, I went swiftly up the stairs.

The landing was only dimly lit, their bedroom door was open, I edged round it, and to my horror saw someone standing there, so close and so near that I banged hard against him; I heard myself cry out, seconds before a hand came over, gently over my mouth, and a voice I knew cautioned me to be quiet. He began to move forward and out of the room, tugging me behind him. It was James, of course. Who else would it be? It was James looking after his sons. 'They're sound asleep, would you believe,' he said against my mouth. And then he kissed me, lightly and sweetly and deeply and hungrily, and I kissed him back. I kissed him back, and I thought of no one but us, I thought of nothing and no one, I latched my arms round his neck. I left the world, I spun to the stars with James. But the landing was hardly a private place, and he let me go at once, as we heard the thud of approaching footsteps, and turned our heads to the sound. I felt guilt and elation all mixed up, but mostly and mainly elation, a kind of euphoria, and I found myself staring in a daze of happiness at Angela Tell as she rounded the bend in the stairs.

She saw nothing amiss, but then why should she? She assumed, as had been the case, that James and I had come to check on the twins. 'Are they all right, sir?'

'Both asleep,' he sounded gruff and abrupt, but improved on this by adding that the children were tough little devils. 'Takes an earthquake to wake them, once they get sound off.'

The three of us went downstairs together. I floated down in a dream. I daren't look at James, I couldn't speak; Donald Cater asked me to dance. James went off with Angela, then I saw him with Aunt Meg, whilst I danced a waltz with Uncle John, bouncing off his stomach, and agreeing with him that the party was a success.

I kept seeing James, on and off, all evening, but he didn't come anywhere near me. I felt he was avoiding me, for in the ordinary way, surely he would have asked me for a duty dance at least. I was his host's niece, he *should* have asked me to dance.

Just before the party broke up I escaped into the garden. I was hot and tired, I felt I needed some air. I went and stood by the boundary fence, the one on the cliff edge. There was no moon and the sea looked solid—dark, and heavy, and heaving. I shivered a little. I wished I had brought a wrap. I turned and looked back at the house, its outline sharply etched against the night sky of riding clouds, its veranda strung with lights. I could see the flit of dancing couples as they moved across the windows. Then I saw one solitary figure emerge from all the rest. And I knew it was James, I knew his build, his walk, and the set of his head. He was crossing the veranda, running down the steps, then the line of shrubs hid him from sight. What was he doing? Where was he going? Was he looking for Ruth? Then he reappeared a few yards from me: 'Ah, *there* you are,' he said. He lifted a hand, the other carried a shawl. 'You'll need this, it's chilly.' He draped it round my shoulders. It smelled of pot-pourri. I wound my arms in it.

'It's Aunt Meg's.'

'She sent me with it.'

'Oh dear, I'm very sorry.'

'Don't be. I was willing to come, very willing indeed!' He was standing close, he moved even closer. I felt his hands cup my face, and lift it slightly, I felt the caress of his thumbs. 'You're so lovely, Thea . . . so appealing . . . you tear the heart out of a man!' His words were thrilling, his touch was magic, my flesh leaned to his hands. Yet I moved away, I made myself move, I stepped backwards and nearly fell. I turned to flee, then heard his voice, quiet, controlled, behind me: 'You don't have to run, there's no need for that. And don't forget this.' I saw him swoop down and pick up the shawl from the ground. I took it from him, mumbling thanks. He didn't help me arrange it, just watched me getting all tangled up, it was one of the loose lacey sort. We began to walk towards the house, and he didn't say a word.

'James.' I swung round, 'I know it's a party, but even counting that, I don't want to do . . . I shouldn't feel right if . . .'

'Leave it, for heaven's sake! Go and join your partner and enjoy yourself, that's what parties are for. Here he is now.' Hugh was coming down the steps. The Reenhams were trailing after him, they attached themselves to James. He was taking them home, and they wanted to go. Old Mrs Reenham was tired. She was having another sneezing fit, and the bursts of raucous noise sloughed through my head like exploding bombs.

Uncle John and Aunt Meg were saying goodnight to several departing guests, including the Caters, Eileen Frewin and Mr Martineau. Ruth had come out of the house with her coat, she joined James and the

Reenhams. The terrace emptied, cars drew off—one of them James's black Rover. I could see Ruth's pale blonde head in the back, she was sitting with Elspeth Reenham; old Mrs Reenham was placed in front with James. I watched them go, watched the car draw away. I felt utterly desolate. I felt as though everything I ever wanted was trickling through my fingers, like fine sand; I jumped when I heard Hugh's voice:

'Penny for them! No, don't bother, let's go in and dance.'

And why not, why not, I thought, after all it *is* a party. So we went off into the sitting-room, where Neil Pardon and Angela Tell, and roughly a dozen other couples were moving over the floor, *just* moving. Neil had his eyes half-closed: 'Good thing it's not "Waltzing Matilda", or he'd be flat on his face.' Hugh gave him an elbow jab as we passed.

It was midnight before everyone went. Hugh stayed to help clear up, so did Miss Tell; she left half an hour later, roaring off in her Mini. She would fetch the twins at breakfast-time, she said.

'Many hands make light work of the chores,' Aunt Meg remarked, looking round the tidy kitchen, once all the clutter was gone, and the dish-washer started its final sluice of the night. Uncle was already in bed, Aunt Meg intended to follow; she crossed the kitchen and said goodnight to Hugh: 'Drive carefully, darling.' She kissed him.

'I always do,' he said. We watched her going up the stairs, shoes off, hand on the rail. Her step was heavy. Aunt Meg was feeling her age: 'She's dead on her feet,' Hugh said reflectively.

'We all are,' I replied. I was rinsing the more fragile

glasses under the running tap. He came behind me and put his arms round my waist.

'I've hardly seen you all evening, not properly, that is. Let's make some coffee and take it through into the sitting-room.'

'It's too late.' I tried to move, but he turned me round to face him. Standing so close I could see every feature— the texture of his skin, light brown eyes with their silky lashes, the heavy black moustache. The eyes had an anxious, sharp look; they put me on my guard. I remembered the way they had looked that day in the shop when I'd broken the vases. I had never quite forgotten that venomous glance.

'What would you say if I asked you to marry me?' he said, letting go of my waist. And I breathed in deeply, and laughed a little, for this was typical Hugh—playing 'just suppose' in the middle of the night.

'I would say "no", much to your relief. We've sparred around this one before, you know perfectly well you don't want to marry me.'

'Ah, but you see I do.' He pushed me down on a wheelback chair, sat on the table in front, swinging his legs, watching me, fingering his moustache. 'I *do* want to marry you, Thea. I'm not fooling, this is for real.'

I stared at him open-mouthed for seconds, probably even minutes. He was serious, I could see he was, he wasn't playing games. He wasn't playing some silly prank, and he wasn't made rash by drink. He never drank—well, very little—he was practically an abstainer; drink wasn't one of his weaknesses. So what must I say, what must I say? How could I put my answer: 'We don't love one another, Hugh.' The truth was the best in the end. He must see that. But apparently he did not:

'Of course we love one another. You've always loved me, Thea.'

'No, Hugh.'

His brow creased, but he went on talking hard: 'And since I've been back from the States I've seen that you're the girl I want. You're beautiful and you're fun too. You're steady, and decent, and helpful. There's nothing you and I couldn't do together. Why, we'd be . . .'

'Oh, Hugh, please stop! Please stop! Please stop!' I had to shout him down. 'I love your companionship, truly I do. You're simply great to be with. But of course we can't marry, you know we can't. It would never, ever work. We get along on the surface perhaps, but underneath we're different . . . we're different people. You must, you must see that!'

He stared at me without speaking for what seemed eternity, his bottom lip caught under his teeth, a pulse flicking hard in his jaw: 'You're overwrought, overtired.' I could see the shape of his fist pushing inside the pocket of his black velvet jacket. I heard him swallow. He seemed to be holding his breath: 'We'll talk about it again sometime. I don't give up easily. You're the girl I want, in every respect. You're *exactly* what I want. And make no mistake, Theadora,' he smiled and flicked my cheek, 'I do love you, very much indeed.'

But he doesn't, I thought, as I watched him go, watched him get in the car, and blow me a kiss, and zoom off down the drive. He doesn't. I closed the door, locked up and went to bed. Hugh was no kind of actor. What he felt showed on his face. And what he didn't feel showed as well, was conspicuous by its absence. His eyes when he'd looked at me hadn't been loving; they had held an eagerness, and a kind of cool calculation, like someone doing sums. He was acquisitive, which must be a plus in his kind of job, especially when teamed with his shrewd ability to see a long way ahead. He knew what he wanted and he seized all his chances, like plucking them off a tree. He liked money—well, we all like it—but Hugh had a touch of avarice. Unflattering though the thought was, I couldn't help wondering if one of the reasons, the main one perhaps, why he'd asked me to marry him, was because of what was contained in Aunt Meg's will.

CHAPTER EIGHT

I HAD the following morning (Friday) off, but got to the Unit at noon, just in time to help with ward lunches before I went to the canteen. Miss Reenham was there, at a table by herself, I made my way over to join her. No sooner had I sat down and begun on my tongue and salad than she started off in praise of the barbecue. 'It was such a treat for my mother, Miss Westering. She doesn't get out very much.'

'I'm glad, I mean, I'm glad she enjoyed it. I think most people did. They seemed to, anyway, and the weather was on our side, not like today.' A gale was blowing—a force-eight south-westerly; my car had rocked as I'd driven along the coast road.

'There's some for whom it had rather unfortunate repercussions, I gather.' She looked at me a little slyly. 'Don't tell me you haven't heard.'

'I've only just come.' What did she mean? What was she getting at? I was soon to know. She was bursting to let it out.

'James Mayling and Sister Filey have broken off their engagement. There's to be no wedding. And, no, it's not gossip. *He* told Sir John, in my hearing, in my presence; there was no question of secrecy.'

'What . . . exactly did he say?' I nearly dropped my knife.

'Just that he and Filey had decided not to marry, he looked rather tense, I thought. The place is buzzing with

126

it. I've seen it coming, though. I told you so, remember?'

'I'm sorry to hear it,' I said, trying my hardest to hide the shock her words had given me. Not even to myself dare I analyse what I really felt inside. Not engaged, not getting married? I longed to ask questions galore. But had I done so, Elspeth Reenham, who was nobody's fool, would have wondered why my interest was so keen.

'He hasn't the same need to get married now, has he?' she said, looking sideways at me, as I tried to swallow my food. Somehow or other I couldn't chew, all my processes seemed to have locked. I drank some water and listened to her remarks: 'He's got a good housekeeper this time, so his home problem's sorted out. His children are being well looked after, his mother won't have to come back. He most likely feels more free and easy than he has done for years. Even so, something must have happened between them last night—probably only a little thing, just the last straw, as it were.'

I felt worse then ever. I jerked and flopped water down my shirt. Had Ruth seen James and me together, outside the twins' room, or even in the garden? Yes, she might have seen us there.

'Do you know who broke it off?' I asked quickly, blurting out the words. Miss Reenham's eyes flashed blue at me, her lips gave a little twist.

'Well, *hardly*, but I can't see *her* saying the fatal words!'

'No,' I said, and then, somehow or other, the full enormity of what we were discussing broke over me in a flood. 'We shouldn't be talking about them like this. It's nothing to do with us.' And no doubt I sounded smug and self-righteous, for she gave a snorting laugh.

'Cast your eye around you,' she said, 'there are sixty tables in here, and I've no doubt at all that over at least forty-five of them, James Mayling's broken engagement is being discussed.'

She was probably right at that, I thought. Hospitals love to gossip. Any enclosed community does; it's meat and drink to gossip. But there was no doubt about it, the species of hospital grapevine was the most tenacious, the most far-reaching there was.

I saw Ruth when I went back downstairs, and my insides gave a lunge, but she didn't look any different from usual, just as trim and neat, and crisply curled, and freckled across the nose. She was so *pretty* . . . she really was pretty . . . a pretty competent woman. She remarked on the party, then off she went to lunch. I suppose the news *is* true, I thought. Miss Reenham's not had a brainstorm? But I had no time to dwell on this, as a new patient arrived. His name was Derek Sompting, and he was shown into my office whilst I filled in the admission details which would start off his folder of notes. He was in for a Bankhart's repair, after a fall from a horse. His left shoulder had been dislocated, and the trouble kept recurring. I find it most inconvenient,' he told me. 'I'm keen on sport, you know . . . cricket, swimming, the odd game of tennis, not to mention my riding.' I sympathised and wrote part of this down in his notes. 'They said I'd be in here about six weeks, perhaps as much as seven. Seems a very long time for a simple thing like a repair.'

'But "repair" is just the medical word for it, Mr Sompting,' I smiled. 'There's a good deal of re-attaching to be done, even though it's a simple op. You'll need to wear a sling and firm bandages for some weeks. Still, I know you'll have heard all this before, from Mr Mayling in Out-patients.'

'He explained it, yes, but one always hopes there's a shorter way round a problem,' he said, looking glum, and nodding his head. He had a bulging forehead and not much chin, and simply enormous feet. They were in tight lace-up shoes which were far too narrow for him. The next thing he'll be in for will be a bunionectomy, I thought, as I took him into the ward.

When I got back I found Susan in my room, adjusting her cap. She wheeled round from the mirror at my approach. 'You'll have heard about the broken romance?'

'Miss Reenham told me at lunchtime.'

'What do you make of it?'

'I don't know.' I sat down at the desk.

'Bang goes my chance of promotion, for she won't leave now, and all right, so I'm selfish. I ought to be thinking of *her*.'

'She may still leave,' I said. 'It won't be easy for her; I mean if she's fond of him, to have to keep seeing him, day after day, would be awful.'

'She's got to get another post first,' Susan said gloomily, just as Nurse Kyle beckoned from the ward.

I began to copy an X-ray report, which Neil Pardon had left on my desk. I was just underlining the first heading when James's head appeared round the door. It appeared high up because of his height, his hair was slightly ruffled; he didn't look altogether in control of the situation. He looked as though he had a lot on his mind. 'I'm slipping in to see Sompting. I take it he *has* arrived?'

'Yes, half an hour since. I took his details.'

'Good. I'll have them, please.' He came slowly into the room. And then I could see the whole of him—head, face, shoulders, tie, white coat, dark trouser legs. My eyes slid up from his shoes to his hands dangling from his cuffs. I went on staring at them. I couldn't look up again. 'Can I have those details please, Thea?'

I jumped at the sound of his voice. 'Yes, of course. I'm sorry, I'm dreaming, I haven't got over last night.' And mentioning last night made me feel worse. Why on earth had I brought that up? I went hot and cold, as I crossed the room, and gave him the folder of notes. Again I tried to meet his eyes and failed.

'What's the matter?'

I stared at his tie. 'Nothing at all,' I said.

'Well, there obviously is. Come and sit down.'

I did so, in front of my desk, I held on to it, both thumbs gripping its edge. He was behind it, standing behind it, spinning my typing chair, with his free hand, I could feel the draught it made. 'I think perhaps you've heard the headline news of the day, and are wondering whether you ought to mention it.'

That wasn't precisely what I was wondering, but I nodded and looked at him. I looked at him straightly and began to feel better at once. Eye contact was everything, without it one felt adrift. 'I would just like to say . . .' I began, then stopped as he held up his hand.

'Please don't say you're sorry,' he said, 'we don't need condolences. It's a broken engagement, not a bereavement, it's an old break too.'

I couldn't think what he meant by that. He made it sound like a fracture. But he plainly wanted all talk of it to cease. 'I'm on leave as from Monday next, for two weeks,' he continued. 'Neil will take over from me. It'll be good experience for him. I shall be at home for the first week, away for the second.'

'I hope you enjoy it.' We were back to banalities. I watched him go on to the ward. I saw Ruth join him; they went to the patient's bed. I had seen them like that so many times, working side by side together, doing their separate, yet complementary jobs. What had happened to part them in private, *if* they had parted, of course. They might just have agreed not to tie the marital knot.

Aunt Meg filled in one or two gaps when I got home that evening. She had been to the hotel to see Helen, and the two of them had talked. 'I could hardly believe it at first, Thea,' she heaped lemon mousse on to my plate. We were having supper, Uncle John was out. 'No, I could hardly believe it. Ruth seemed so right for James. She seemed right for the children too, which had to count, of course. And Helen was . . . *is* very fond of her.'

'Do you know what happened?' I spooned up my mousse. It was very, very tart. It wrung my mouth. I listened to Aunt Meg's words.

'Well, according to Helen, James and Ruth have had differences for some time.'

'You mean, quarrels?'

'I don't think quite that, just strong disagreements, Helen said they steered a checkered course.'

'What finally broke them up, then?'

'Just second thoughts, Helen said. They made the decision not to marry three days after her attack.'

I stared at her for a second or two. 'Seven weeks ago. You mean when we'd got the twins here, when Helen was so ill! Heavens, Aunt Meg, what a funny time to choose!'

She smiled and tucked a strand of hair back behind her ear. 'Occasionally, darling, shock happenings bring things to a head, force out truths which can prove unpalatable, which *might* have happened in their case. They didn't make the news generally known because of Helen's condition. They waited until they felt she could take it with reasonable calm; they told her last night, just before they came here.'

'I see,' I said, and then I was silent. I was thinking back over that time, back to Helen's heart attack, to James's edginess, and also, to Elspeth Reenham's remarks. 'Do they still see each other,' I asked, 'out of hours, I mean?'

'I could hardly enquire about that, could I?' Aunt Meg looked a little surprised. 'What she didn't tell me, I couldn't dig for. I would think, though, that they don't. I noticed James looking rather lost, several times last evening. I sent him out to join *you* once.'

My face began to scorch. I had never been so glad to hear the slam of a car door, nor to see Uncle John's portly figure crossing the tussocky lawn, for it made a diversion just when I needed one most.

The gossip over the broken engagement lapsed during the following week. Ruth never mentioned it once to me, which probably wasn't surprising. We had seldom talked with any closeness, nor talked very much at all. And after three whole months on the Unit I didn't feel I knew her any better than when I had first come through the doors.

It was a humdrum week, with few excitements. James, of course, was on leave. Neil Pardon came on to the ward twice, sometimes three times a day. Miss Reenham

said Vinton Ward had him there as well. He was naturally very anxious that nothing should go wrong; so with
out-patients' clinics, and the wards, and theatre, his life
was very full. He lost weight too, through the toil of his
sixteen-hour day. 'But I keep bobbing up,' he told me,
'I'm in very good heart, Miss Westering. Orthopaedic
surgery is my *métier*, I'm sure. I'm to stand in on that
bone-grafting operation on Monday—the patient with
the osteoid osteoma.' His words sprayed out; he had
small square teeth with a whistle-gap.

'It should be worth seeing,' I watched him wipe his
mouth. 'And a bone-graft patient is a very interesting
nursing case as well.' The patient we were discussing was
a young man of nineteen. He had a tumour on his shin
which had caused the bone to split. The tumour (a
benign type) would be removed, but a bone graft would
be necessary to fill the gap and encourage new healthy
bone formation. The whole procedure was very
intricate.

'Presumably the donor site will be the iliac fossa, the
crest of the hip-bone, don't you think?'

I said that I thought it would. What I was really
thinking, or wishing, was that Neil would go. He had
handed over the letters and reports he wanted me to
type. They were all written out in longhand, for he
couldn't dictate, he said. It flustered him, he liked to
write things down. I didn't mind, for his handwriting was
large and clear, like him, but he always brought it along
so late, and I seldom caught the post. When James was
here, he hurried him up, so from that point of view I
missed him. The relief I had thought I would feel in his
absence was wearing a little thin. I wanted to see him,
and that was why on Sunday afternoon I deliberately

walked along the Undercliff as far as the harbour. He might be there, he might not, but I knew he owned a boat, and I knew her name; she was called *Valkyrie*. Aunt Meg had told me that. Aunt Meg and her friendship with Helen was useful stuff.

I sat on the wall, and scanned the boats. I spotted *Valkyrie* at once. She was a sailing-cruiser—blue and silver and cream. She bobbed at her mooring, she gleamed in the sunlight, and someone was on board. I saw a movement in the cabin, then out through the hatch came a man. Was it James? Yes, of course it was James, in a peaked sailing cap, and an old jersey, and loose-fitting, turned-up jeans. His back was to me, he was lugging a rope, a heavy coil of it. He began to drag it over the foredeck; it was then that he looked across—across and up—and saw me on the wall. 'Why *hello*, there!' he snatched off his cap. Three boats divided us, and bobbed between us. I got down from the wall.

'What a lovely boat.'

'Yes, isn't she. Come and look over her. That's the best way to get down, I think.' Six steps led to the jetty, he pointed them out, I skimmed down like a bird. Once alongside *Valkyrie*, I took his outstretched hand and stepped on board, adjusting to the movement beneath my feet.

My parents had owned a boat for some years before they went abroad. I had sailed with them often, Father had taught me to crew. So I knew what James meant when he talked about a well-flared bow, and explained the rigging. I inspected everything.

'She's a super boat, simply terrific.'

'You a good sailor?' he asked.

That gave me my chance: 'Well, I used to be.' I shaded

my eyes from the glare. 'I used to crew for my father when we came down here at weekends. We had a sloop, Bermudan rigged.'

'So you know how to sail?'

'Yes.'

He was taking the covers off: 'Like to come out now, I wonder . . . just for a little way? Of course you may be pushed for time?'

My heart began to beat fast. Then, well, why not, I thought? What harm could it do, what possible harm, and the weather was exactly right for sailing. A brisk south-westerly wind was blowing, the clouds were cotton-wool puffs. I was wearing jeans, and a shirt and sweater; I would manage all right in those. 'I'd love to come,' I told him, smiling. He turned me towards the cabin.

'Find yourself another jersey. There's one of mine in the locker. Meanwhile, I'll cast off.' He stepped nimbly on to the quay. By the time I got back on deck in a jersey long enough for a mini-skirt we were moving out of the harbour mouth under power.

Once out, and into the wind, he switched the engine off, and hoisted the sails, then came back to the helm. 'No boy-friend today?' he stared straight ahead.

'No, not today,' I replied. 'We don't live in each other's pockets.'

'I think that's very wise.' And now he was being enigmatic; yes, even out at sea. The boat heeled and I slid across the seat. 'And how's life on the Unit?' I felt him look down at me, and the thought crossed my mind that he hadn't seen Ruth or she would have told him about it. Such a little thing to make me happy, but I fairly brimmed with it.

'Nothing very startling has happened, but you can't want to know about work.'

'It's not all that easy to forget it, you know, not whilst I'm here in the area. I've been taking the boys out and about. We went to Town on Wednesday. We went to the Zoo, which enchanted them, but had me on my knees. I understand that your aunt and uncle will be up in Town next Saturday to celebrate their anniversary, their wedding anniversary.'

'Their silver wedding, their twenty-fifth, twenty-five years married. They're setting off at breakfast-time, having lunch at the Savoy, then going to a theatre matinee, having drinks with friends, then home again, before midnight strikes, they say.'

'They're a very happy couple.'

'They're still in love,' I said. 'They're not just suitably married, they can still surprise one another; they're not dull, they've kept their marriage alive. It's my aunt's second marriage too, her first husband died, so it just goes to show.' I stopped then, aware of what I was saying. What must he think of me, nattering on like that.

He smiled and gave a little nod, but didn't make any comment. And for some time after that, apart from the slap of the sea, and the whistling sound of the wind in the rigging, there was silence on the boat. It was a silence that was broken by James, talking about his leave. 'I'm off to Cornwall tomorrow,' he said, 'returning late Friday night. I'm not back on duty till Monday officially, but I promised Sir John that I'd be in the area, on call, all Saturday, just in case of emergencies.'

'Will you sail to Cornwall?'

'No, motor. I shall have the twins with me. I'm taking

them to see their maternal grandparents, who are back in England for good.'

'How long is it since they have seen the boys?'

'They saw them last year. They were in England then, looking for a house. I helped them secure a plot. I know the district fairly well. My birthplace was Cornwall. My father was a lecturer at Meltravissen University. I grew up within sight and sound of the sea.'

'Do you ever bring the twins sailing?'

'Oh yes, whenever I can, but I keep them in life-jackets *and* harnesses, and clip them to the rail. I daren't take chances, not with two slippery eels like them. In another two years or so, I hope to teach them to crew, especially Barty, who shows signs of being keen. William's more for dry land, for gardening, making things grow. There's a lot of my wife in William, she used to spend hours in the garden. Most of the lilacs at Northbarn were planted by Val.'

This was the second time he had mentioned his dead wife to me. I wondered if he might tell me more, I liked the sound of her, but he went on to ask me about my parents, and commented on their work. 'I've read most of your father's books, and I once saw him on television, in an interview with Ruston Blane. Your mother was there as well.'

'They're a glamorous couple, and wonderful parents. They live in Ibiza now, at a small place called Ca'n Furnet. They do all their writing there.'

'You're not tempted to join them?'

'Not in the least. I prefer to nurse in England. I would *quite* like to go to America, but only for a time. Hugh liked it at first, but only for the useful experience, he said. Hugh's the type who prefers to be a big frog in a small pool. Lowhampton is exactly right for him, being fairly near to London.'

'To visit you?'

'I doubt if he'll do much of that,' I said. James' eyes met mine, he looked puzzled; he got up to ease the sheets; then he turned the boat to starboard till the wind blew across her beam. And as the sails blew out at a wider angle, a different motion was felt. The boat didn't heel nearly so much, she began to force along. And instead of pitching and tossing, we soared and dipped with a gliding movement. It was blissful, it was sailing at its best.

'It's wonderful, James . . . oh, it's magical . . . marvellous!' I went to stand at his side.

'She's dancing to her own rhythm,' he said. His face was as rapt as mine. And it seemed to me, as I stood there beside him, as though the whole of me danced to him, as though we were in tune. I couldn't sit, I kept at his side, moving with the boat. He kept her on course with the lightest of touches, he seemed to restrain her little. He put an arm about my waist and drew me hard against him. He turned his head, we snatched a kiss, laughed, and broke away. The wind blew my hair out like a banner, James' hand returned to the helm. Yet the kiss, though transitory, bound and entranced us, exactly like a spell; and the world was ours, a world of sea and sky.

'I'm glad you came with me.' We watched a gull mewing overhead. 'It matters whom a man takes to sea—not any girl will do!'

'I'm glad to know I'm sea-worthy!' His compliment meant so much. But keep it light, keep it light, don't fall in love with him, I counselled myself; this is just an interlude. It was easy to get a kind of sea-madness, born of water and breeze. That was all it was, a passing madness, induced by Poseidon and Zephyr. Those wicked old gods had a great deal to answer for. James was attractive, physically compelling. I had known that from our first meeting—that traumatic, collision-course meeting on the train. I had known it, too, at Northbarn, in that lovely home-like house, when I had wanted him near, yet wanted to escape.

And on his side, I attracted him, or at least I did for the moment. He was on holiday—all set and prepared to enjoy what came his way. *I* had come his way today, purposely, with intent. I had sat on the wall, hopefully sat there, willing him to see me, willing him to ask me to step on board. So whatever has happened, I started it off, I thought with a little sigh, watching Dillhaven Harbour swaying in front of my eyes.

His hand left my waist: 'I'll turn now,' he said, 'I don't want to berth here. It's not worth it, not worth tying up, unless we stay for some time.'

I fancied his voice rose a little in query: 'I ought to get back,' I said, 'they'll be expecting me, wondering where I am.'

Once the boat was round, with a following wind, the movement changed again. We rolled in a kind of cork-screw motion, more difficult to control. James' hands were hard and fast on the helm during the journey back, but although we were silent, or nearly so, the atmosphere wasn't strained. He smiled at me every now and then, as I sat there in the stern. He may have been wondering if I felt ill, but praise be I did not. Nothing must spoil this time with him which, so far, had been perfect. I would never forget it, interlude or not.

'We must do this again,' he said when, with sails neatly furled, we were moving into Lowhampton under power.

'Oh yes,' I said, 'yes, I would love to!' But I wondered when it would be. After next weekend there was only one more before I returned to Town. And in any case, he might not mean it. It might be one of those things men often say at the end of a pleasant date.

We were drawing alongside the mooring. He threw the ropes on to the quay, to two youths, who offered to pull us in. I went to the cabin to strip off his jersey, but not before I had seen, up on the wall where I had sat, two little fair-haired boys, together with Angela Tell in a hat like a panama, together with Badger, straining on his lead. We were home, we were back, it was all over, we were on our own no more. I tried in vain to tidy my hair, but stickied by wind and spray it hung about my face in ropey strands. A small mirror over one of the bunks reflected my shiny brown face, festooned by hair, freaked out like a hawthorn hedge. I look like one of the original Raggle-taggle Gypsies-oh, I thought wryly, as the boat gave a little bounce. Seconds later the running thump of feet on deck prepared me for the advent of the twins:

'Behold the family!' James was with them. 'Angela's staying on land, sensible woman.' Barty pushed in front.

'We didn't know you were going with Daddie. If we'd known that *we* could have come, you'd have looked after us.'

'And finished the story about the sailor with the sore foot,' said William.

'Another time,' James told them, getting out of his jersey, stooping to roll down the legs of his jeans.

'Angela's taking us to see Nan now, I expect we'll stay

to supper. Nan's going back to her own house soon, and she's going to have a cat. We like cats, but we like dogs better.' Barty was still sounding off when, out on the deck once more, James lifted him on to the quay. Then it was William's turn, then mine. I must have tested his strength, for although I'm narrow and thin I'm not the ideal length for swinging from boat to shore with any ease.

I said goodbye to them all up on the Undercliff Walk. I was aware of my audience when I took my leave of James. Angela, with Badger under her arm, edged tactfully away. Not so the twins, who wanted to know if I had been seasick, and, 'Did Daddie make you put a life-jacket on?'

'Thank you for coming,' James took my hand, our eyes met and held, and the spell began to weave all over again.

'It's for me to say thank you, it was fabulous.'

'Every drop of the way.'

'I hope you enjoy your few days in Cornwall.'

'I expect I will,' he replied.

I made to withdraw my hand and he let it go, but went on talking. 'Thea, about next Saturday. Could you lunch with me? You may, of course, have other plans, but if not, with your folk away, well, it might break up the day up a bit. I'd enjoy your company.' He brought out the invitation with a certain amount of diffidence, and I so much hated having to turn him down, but I couldn't help it, for Wendy was coming to spend the day with me. I explained this as best I could:

'She's my London flatmate, you see, and we made the arrangement some time ago. She's looking forward to it.'

'Of course. Another time, perhaps. It was just a thought,' he said. 'Until Monday week, then,' he smiled and turned, and went to join the others.

My legs didn't feel as though they matched, as I started the short walk home. The transition from sea to land was harder by far than the other way round, or at least I found it so, but part of my 'drunkenness' might have been due to the way I was feeling . . . high on happiness.

I ought to have known it couldn't possibly last . . .

CHAPTER NINE

AUNT MEG kept bemoaning the fact that Hugh hadn't been in touch: 'You two haven't quarrelled, I hope?' she said on Monday morning, just as I was setting off for work.

'No, we haven't,' I refused to be drawn. 'I expect he's very busy, or away again. You know how it is with Hugh.'

She nodded, but looked unconvinced. She would probably ring him up, or call at the shop, she wouldn't leave things in the air. As for me, I was relieved that he had not asked me out again. I felt that from now on twosomes were out, but I wished he would come to the house. We were both of us 'family', and I knew it would please Aunt Meg.

I had three more weeks to work through, as a ward secretary. After that it was back to London, back to my staff nurse post. I had already heard from the senior nursing officer at St Mildred's, saying how glad she would be to see me back. She had written (for her) quite a fulsome letter: 'You have been greatly missed, Nurse Westering.' There was more in this vein, it was good to be missed, good to be going back. I kept telling myself this very firmly as I drove along the coast road. My real life and work lay up in Town.

Wendy would be here at the weekend. Would I tell her about James? I probably would, for she and I had weathered most things together. We had seen one another through various crisis times.

Lytton Ward was busy that morning. Two patients were due for surgery—Guy Milford, for bone-grafting, and a middle-aged man, Roy Stepton. Mr Stepton had a troublesome elbow, which didn't move freely. Every now and then the joint locked, mostly when his arm was extended; he would be unable to bend it up again. X-ray revealed that part of the rounded end of his humerus had become detached, and had formed a loose body within the elbow joint. It had become very painful and swollen due to serum collecting—synovial effusion, to use the medical term. I knew Uncle John intended to operate to remove the loose fragment. The elbow joint should then be good as new.

'Ruth's on lates,' Susan told me, folding her apron forward and seating herself on the corner of my desk. 'She doesn't seem unduly depressed about her crashed marriage plans.'

'She's not the type to show face, is she? She's the composed sort,' I said.

'She's secretive.' Susan looked annoyed. 'I wish we knew her plans.'

'There's no reason to suppose she'll be going, Susan. I shouldn't count on it. After all, as you said yourself, she's got to get a new post. This is her job, and she may not want to leave.'

'She was with Cecil Mallory, the neurosurgeon, quite a bit, at your party. I couldn't help wondering if there might be a sister's job going at Wellbridge. He's met Ruth before, you know. He operated here last March. We had a child in with a spinal tumour. He and Sir John combined skills. The child was nursed in our side-ward here; Mallory came to visit. So he knows a little about

Ruth, and he's very influential—a clever surgeon, almost as good as Sir John.'

I agreed that he was, but I felt Susan's thoughts bordered on the wishful. Ruth liked her job at St Stephen's, and seemed determined to stick to it—as was her right—and in that I could sympathise. And apart from that, she and James might still have some sort of link-up. I began to type, and blotted them out of my thoughts.

That afternoon Ruth told me a new secretary had been engaged, to take over from me, when I left in three weeks' time. 'We were very lucky to get her,' she said, 'she's the girl James and I wanted at the time you were sent here by Sir John. She's middle-aged and most reliable, more the Eileen Frewin type.'

I wanted to retort that middle-aged types weren't the *only* reliable ones. Instead I said how glad I was. 'You were obviously meant to have her. What a good thing she was still available.'

'James's words exactly,' she smiled and went out of the room. I began to type in angry stabs. Ruth's words rankled. I didn't like her. It was no good saying I did.

The ward was quiet, I noticed later, when I went to the central desk. This was in deference to the two patients recently back from theatre. The bone-graft boy, Guy Milford, had his curtains drawn back. He had been placed in a semi-recumbent position, in an effort to relieve the tension on his donor-site wound—the crest of his hip-bone, which had supplied the graft for his shin. Having two wounds, his would be a long stay, possibly close on four months. He would be glad of some sort of occupational therapy after a time. There were three men in the ward at the moment doing simple tapestry work.

Rugs weren't so easy, unless they were small, and knitting wasn't popular; there was more of that going on in the women's ward.

The week wore on, the weekend drew nearer, I was looking forward to it. It would be so good to see Wendy again, and to hear all the news from St Mildred's. It would prepare me for going back, re-kindle my enthusiasm for work in a London hospital, where I belonged.

But on Thursday evening Wendy telephoned to tell me her visit was off. 'Honestly, Thea, you'll never believe it, but I've gone and contracted mumps. Mumps, I ask you, at my age! I'm in quarantine, of course.'

'Wendy, what rotten luck! Oh, I *am* sorry . . . poor old you!'

'I expect I'll live,' she sounded miserable, 'but my face is out like a ball. I shall be off work for another fortnight, until you get back here. I'm in sick bay, being waited on, so no need to worry.' We talked for a little while longer and then she had to ring off.

When I told Aunt Meg she looked rather vexed, but a little thoughtful too, so I wasn't in the least surprised when she came back from shopping on Friday to tell me that she had seen Hugh, and he might come round on Saturday. 'I told him John and I would be out, and that you could do with some company.'

'Saturday is his busiest day,' I felt quite annoyed with Aunt Meg. The last thing I wanted was a tête-à-tête session with Hugh at The Moorings.

'He's not busy after six o'clock. I expect he'll come then.' She went on to tell me about the play she and Uncle were seeing in London: 'It's *The Dark Divide*, Thea, by Leonard Cruikshank, it's had excellent reviews. And everything comes at once, doesn't it, for next

Thursday, you know, I'm going to the matinee at the Doric Theatre here in Lowhampton, to see *Heartbreak House* with two of my golfing friends.'

'I wouldn't mind seeing that myself.'

'Get Hugh to take you, love.' There was one thing about Aunt Meg, she never gave up.

Saturday dawned, hot and sunny. 'We'll swelter in Town,' Uncle puffed, as he and Aunt Meg climbed into the Lancia, just after breakfast-time.

'Have a super day,' I waved them off. I went back into the house. There was no doubt about it, it felt very strange with no one in it but me. I washed up and did one or two chores, then went down into the village to buy eggs and cheese, and fruit, and salad stuff. I knew I was hoping to run into James. He would have come home from Cornwall last night. But there was no sign of him at the shops, nor of Angela Tell, and I firmly resisted driving up as far as Northbarn House. I couldn't pursue him as obviously as that. What was so tantalising was that, due to Wendy's absence, I could have lunched with him, had that meal out with him, as he'd asked. I could ring him, of course, but I knew I wouldn't, I hadn't got quite enough cheek, for even that would smack of pursuit, and never in my life had I chased a man—except Hugh in foolish youth.

Coming back from the village I swam and lay on the beach till one o'clock. I returned to the house, put my lunch on a tray, and took it into the garden. I ate cheese and biscuits, raspberries and cream, then stretched myself out on the grass. I felt indolent, sleepy, relaxed and warm, comfortably tired from my swim. I could feel sleep taking me over, sounds receded and boomed, in and out like the pull of the tide, a bee's drone filled my

ears. I oughtn't to sleep, but I couldn't resist: I couldn't
. . . couldn't resist. So I let my lids fall and I drifted into a
doze. It was the lightest of dozes, it must have been, for
through the hazy layers, I felt the presence of someone
beside me, I felt someone's gaze upon me, heard the
rustle of grass beside my head. I strove to wake, to break
surface, and when at last I did, I saw only the garden,
bathed in sunlight, the dreaming, quiet house, the sky
above like a sheet of pale blue silk. I sat up, knuckling
my eyes; it must have been a dream. And it hadn't been
very clever of me to go to sleep in the garden, at the
bottom of the garden too, leaving the house wide open.
What kind of a caretaker was I? Thieves could have
walked in, and helped themselves, and then walked out
again. The sensible thing would have been to sit on the
terrace and keep awake. I picked up my tray and began
to walk to the house.

I was still in my towelling beach dress, I was bare-
footed too, so I made no sound, or very little, as I went
up the terrace steps, and entered the house, and stood in
the carpeted hall. And the moment I did so, the second I
came under the hang of the roof, the second the walls
wrapped round me, I knew I wasn't alone. There was
someone there, and as I listened, I heard little rustling
movements. My scalp crawled, the top of my spine went
cold. The sounds came from the sitting-room, and the
door was partly open, not standing wide, but open
enough for me to see one wall, and a strip of carpet, and
the start of the french doors. I moved forward, silently
forward, I set the tray on the stairs. I peered through the
hinge side of the door, I got a good view of the room, and
there by the silver wedding gifts which Aunt Meg had
displayed on a table, was Hugh, looking at one of the

many cards. I felt so relieved I just bounded forward and rushed into the room. He wheeled round and I saw a card flutter from his fingers. He looked at me in astonished anger at first.

'For crying out loud, you might have called out, not pounced on me like that!'

'Oh Hugh, I thought you were a thief! I thought someone had broken in!'

'Walked in, you mean, don't you? All the doors were open! Not very wise of you, Thea, my love.' He smiled, and his startled look faded. He picked the card up from the carpet and put it back in its envelope. He should never have taken it out in the first place, I thought, with a prick of annoyance. It had been one of several that had come after Aunt and Uncle had left for Town. Some of the envelopes hadn't been sealed, they had come with their flaps tucked in. Hugh had a nerve, a colossal cheek to peek and pry inside. I gave him a very straight look, but I didn't say anything. He would only have said there was no harm done and laughed at me for my pains, or got angry again, which I wanted to avoid. 'There's a good motley collection here,' he waved a hand over the presents. 'I called to bring mine.' He pointed to a crystal bowl with a silver rim. 'Think they'll like it?' he passed it over to me.

'I'm sure they will. It's lovely, Hugh,' I felt slightly better towards him. 'And you're right, of course, I shouldn't have left the house wide open. I was in the garden, I went to sleep.'

'Yes, I know. I saw you. I was tempted to wake you up . . . with a kiss, of course.' He turned me round, held me by the shoulders. 'A snazzy dress, bare feet and legs . . . very, *very* sexy!'

'I've been on the beach.'

'Lucky beach!' The blandishment tripped off his tongue. I didn't believe what he said, either. He hadn't intended to wake me. He had hoped I would sleep for longer, maybe. He had seized the opportunity to come in here, and have a look round, and peek and pry a little. There was no real harm in him, but he liked to know about people, and what they had got, and to put a price on their things. 'I've got to return to the shop,' he said, 'but I'll come back this evening. I promised Meg I would keep you company.'

'There's no need. I'm all right on my own.'

'Independent Thea!' He lifted a strand of my hair and laid it over my mouth and chin. 'I want to come. I've not seen you for ages. I'll cook omelettes for supper. We'll play records, settle down like Darby and Joan.'

'I doubt if Darby and Joan listened to LPs,' I laughed, just as a step sounded outside and a shadow slipped over the carpet. I was fairly certain whose shadow it was, even before I turned. Framed in the french windows with the sun raying out behind him, was James with a small gift-wrapped box in his hand. 'James . . . hello.' I stood and smiled, feeling as I always did, at the sight of him, a push of gladness, a rush of happiness. He was here. He had come to see me. I heard Hugh greeting him, over-doing the welcome, inviting him into the room.

'Hello, Thea,' he looked straight at me, and handed me the box. 'For Sir John and Lady Westering, with my best wishes,' he said.

'How kind of you.' To my great annoyance Hugh and I spoke together, giving a false impression of rapport.

'Considering all they've done for me, it's a small return,' James said.

'Well, of course, if you put it like that, old man.' Oh, why didn't Hugh shut up?

'I *do* put it like that,' James's face gave little away. It was polite in expression, even unconcerned, but dismay swept over me, as in thought I changed places with him, as in thought I stood where he stood, saw myself with Hugh's arm about me, saw my miniscule dress, my bare legs, my untidy hair. Heavens, what must he think! He had expected to find Wendy here. I had told him she was coming. I had turned down his invitation to lunch all because of Wendy. He had called here with a gift for my aunt, and had found me with Hugh. Yes, found me with Hugh, that's what it would look like, that's what it would look like to him, as though I had lied, made the Wendy visit up.

'I must go.' Hugh kissed the top of my head, and made for the door. 'I'll be back at seven, or soon after, just as soon as I can.'

'I must go too,' James stepped from the room. He practically followed Hugh out.

'Did you enjoy your few days in Cornwall? Did everything go off well?' I wanted to stop him, delay him, explain. I itched to catch hold of his arm, and drag him back, and make him listen to me.

'Yes,' he said shortly. His car, like Hugh's, was parked in the road. Hugh's zoomed away, James started to walk down the drive.

'James . . .'

'Yes?' He stopped and turned round, and I blenched at the look in his eyes. Not that they accused, they didn't; they were simply politely enquiring, almost opaque, and hard as pebble-stones.

'My friend, Wendy, has contracted mumps, so of

course she couldn't come.'

'Oh dear, I'm sorry to hear that. There's a lot of it about.' He gave a little 'goodbye' salute, and walked down to his car. In no way did he hurry off, but there was something about his gait, and the set of his shoulders, that warned me to stay exactly where I was. He had the kind of manner and bearing that could quell without a word. I made no attempt to follow him down the drive.

I went to the kitchen and gulped at some water, standing up by the sink. James hadn't believed me, at best he'd been sceptical. Why should I care what he thought? But oh, how I wished I had been on my own when he came tapping on the glass. Oh, how I wished that Hugh had been somewhere else.

True to his word Hugh arrived back at The Moorings just after seven. By then I had changed into jeans and a shirt, and washed and tied back my hair. He cooked herb omelettes, and I made a salad. We ate our repast in the kitchen. Omelettes, Hugh said, disliked being carted about.

'If you hadn't been an antiques dealer you could have got a job as a chef,' I told him, 'and opened a restaurant.'

'A bistro?'

'Mm, that's right.'

'There's more money in antiques.' He laughed and whisked my plate away, and began to peel me a peach. I was getting the full treatment. I couldn't help wondering why. Over coffee and Turkish Delight (the latter having been brought by Hugh), I found out. And I couldn't believe my ears. We were in the sitting-room at the time, sitting comfortably on the settee. Hugh led up to his point by stealthy degrees.

'Thea, I know you don't want to marry me, you've

made that pretty plain. I was going to try to, well, to persuade you, but I think I'd be wasting my time. What I'm trying to get round to saying is that I hope we can be friends.'

Foolishly I began to relax, to think to myself, 'thank goodness'. 'I'm glad you've brought it up,' I said. 'I would hate not to be friends. It would upset Aunt Meg too. She looks upon us as her children. She's as good as said so. She watches over us!'

'She's told you about her will, I expect?' Hugh was drinking his coffee. His lashes were down, his nose was in the cup.

'Yes, she explained it to me several weeks ago, about Allan's fund. It's good of her to think of us like that.'

'Godchildren are usually left something in wills.' His cup went down with a clink. He took mine from me and set them down on a nearby table. I think it was about then that I began to get warning prickles, to sense that Hugh had a good deal more to say. 'In addition to being a godchild,' he went on, 'I'm a close blood relative. Meg is my mother's sister. One can't get much closer than that. And also I remember Uncle Allan, only vaguely, of course. He was a boatbuilder, I used to play in his yard.' There was a pause, and I think he probably expected some sort of comment from me, but my warning prickles were growing in size, I half-guessed what was coming. I wasn't going to make things easier for Hugh; he must say what he had to without any help from me. His next remark was a question—a fairly direct one, too. 'Thea,' he turned to me, taking one of my hands in his, 'don't you think that to leave Allan's money divided equally between us, is unfair to me, bearing all this in mind?'

'What's unfair about equal parts?' I said when I could

utter. At first I couldn't, he had taken my breath away.

'In my case it's especially unfair. I have no other expectations. My mother's got nothing very much, what she has will go to her paramour.' His lip curled, his expression was ugly, he talked like a jealous child. 'Whereas you, you're differently placed, aren't you? Your parents are doing well, making money out of their books, and you're their only child. I think Meg should have seen to it that I had a larger proportion—at least three-quarters of Allan's fund.'

I pulled my hand away from his. I expect my face was a study, for he said very quickly: 'Don't you agree, or am I putting it badly?'

'Boldly, is how I'd describe it.'

'But don't you agree that I'm right?'

'I haven't thought very much about it, but obviously *you* have. The last time I thought about it at all was when you proposed to me. That's why you proposed, isn't it, Hugh? Because I'm a good catch, or will be one day when the people I love are dead.'

'That wasn't the only reason.'

'But it had to do with it.'

He ignored that, and looking at him, I could see he hadn't finished. He was busy framing his next sentence which, when spoken, left me aghast. 'There's time for Meg to change her will. She would, if you asked her to. You could put it to her, stress how I'm placed. Say it's been bothering you.'

'You must be crazy!'

'You know I'm not.'

'Well, then you've got a nerve! You're the one with the sway with Aunt Meg. If you want the will changed, *you* ask.' Do your own dirty work, I added under my breath.

'She would think I was grasping.'

'She'd be right, wouldn't she?' I got up from the settee. 'You're calculating, Hugh, dis—dismayingly so. You've taken my breath away.' I had to escape, I went on to the patio.

'If you approached her, she'd do it,' he said, following me out. 'I know it's a funny thing to ask.'

'You can say that again!'

'But I felt I could ask it of you.'

'In the name of friendship, you mean?'

'Out of affection too, Thea. You loved me once, remember. You told me once, standing not so far from where we are standing now, that you'd do anything for me, anything in the world.'

'That was schoolgirl's talk.'

'You're the same girl, fair-minded and straight. Think about it. I've my way to make. It's different for a man.'

'So I've heard.'

'Will you ask her? Will you try to help?'

'I don't think I can,' I said. 'I wish Aunt Meg hadn't mentioned her will to either of us, Hugh. I hated it when she was speaking about it. I can't bring it up again. I can't ask her, I don't want to, for all sorts of reasons!'

He was watching me closely, and I knew why, I also knew what he saw. I was objecting, but objecting too much; my vehemence showed my weakness. He knew there was a hope, a chance, that I might do as he asked. 'Sleep on it,' he said easily. 'Think it over, darling. In the meantime, forget it. We'll go out, if you like.'

So the subject was dropped, just for the moment, but it wasn't out of mind. Hugh hadn't let go of it, he would bring it up again. He would bring it up, draw it up, like a bucket out of a well; I worried about it when I got to bed that night.

The things he said were true too: he *was* a close relative, much closer than me, and my parents were comfortably off. But how could I mention all this to Aunt Meg? She knew it, anyway. She would guess Hugh had put me up to it. She would think me a silly fool. It was at this point that my worry thinned. I sat up and put on the light. That's what I was—a silly fool—not to have realised that of course Aunt Meg would have given due thought to all these points herself. She would have taken Hugh's circumstances (and mine) into consideration. She had made the bequest as she *wanted* to make it, and of course she mustn't change it. I couldn't ask her. Why should I? It wouldn't be right.

As I switched off the light and lay down again I realised how drained I felt. Indecision is like a storm, it blows one hither and thither. But once a firm course is decided upon, a kind of quietness follows. In the quiet after the 'Hugh storm' I began to think of James. Perhaps, on Monday, I would have a chance to talk to him properly, perhaps to explain . . .

Most of all, to explain.

CHAPTER TEN

I WAS filing at the ward desk when he came to do the round. From where I sat I could hear a good deal of what was going on, as he went from bed to bed, accompanied by Ruth. He acknowledged me by a little nod, as he came through the doors. He didn't smile, and neither did I; I bent my head to my papers, I swallowed hard and tried to concentrate.

One got a different view of him—here in the ward—as he halted, and bent over beds, frowned over charts and notes. Several patients were ambulant, and he watched their progress on crutches, or Zimmers, or walking frames, or sticks.

Watching him flex the leg of a footballer who had had a meniscectomy, I was reminded of that Sunday morning, nearly four months ago, when I had keeled over on the Undercliff Walk, and he had come to my rescue, and examined my knee with gentle expertise. He seemed different now. *Was* he different? I knew him better, of course. He was straightening up, and from my seat in the centre of the ward, I noted afresh the brown of his skin, and the way it crinkled and folded in little lines, whenever he smiled or laughed.

The patients seemed glad to see him back. They enquired about his holiday. They talked to him over plastered limbs, over high cervical collars, through pulleys and ropes, from hoists and ripple-beds.

Paul Merrick (the university student whose drip I had

157

once re-started) had made good progress, and was anxious to be discharged. I heard James tell him he would need to be patient for a few weeks longer. Paul was having daily physiotherapy.

Mr Roland Flint, an arthritic, who had had surgery on his toes, was asked to swing his legs over the side of his bed. His feet were examined, James asked him to stand, which he did with much grunting and groaning. His feet had a strange appearance, as his toes were raised by pads which had been fixed to his soles with Elastoplast:

'Try to push your toes downwards,' James urged, 'push to get them down.' Mr Flint tried, but kept complaining of pain. 'You must try to walk through the discomfort,' James was very firm. 'Your pain is due to cut bones; they are bound to hurt at first. Now, let go of Sister, take your stick, and try to walk on your own.' He shuffled a few steps, James applauded him. 'There you are, you see, you can do it, but try to raise your feet higher, don't shuffle, lift them up. Splendid, that's the way. Yes, I know they hurt, but as each day passes the pain will get less and less. Okay, all right, that's enough for now.'

Ruth helped him back to bed. I saw her summon Nurse Kyle, and ask her to get the patient a drink. 'Tea, Nurse, and a chocolate biscuit, the wafer sort Mr Flint likes.' Her mothering nature was much in evidence. James smiled at her, I saw him. My throat went tight. I was sure he still cared for her.

'He may want his freedom, but he still keeps very close company with Ruth Filey,' Elspeth Reenham said at lunchtime, when she joined me in the canteen. 'His car was on the park outside her flat all Saturday evening, *and* most of Saturday night as well.'

'Do you keep a round-the-clock vigil?' I asked. Her glasses misted over.

'It just so happened that I had to get up to Mother in the night. I don't spy on people, but I do have a right to look out of my own windows.'

'I'm sorry,' I said. There was no need to take out my feelings on her. But what she said confirmed what I thought. James still cared for Ruth. There was something left, perhaps a good deal, they might just have agreed a new basis. That afternoon on the boat when he had seemed to care for me hadn't meant very much. It had been a type of holiday romance—a short-short version, like the stories in magazines.

His gift to my aunt and uncle had been a pair of tiny salt-cellars in silver-gilt, shaped like little boats. They had been delighted with them. I knew Uncle John had thanked him, but later that afternoon when James was with me in the office, Aunt Meg rang up to make sure he was thanked again. We were in the middle of dictation when the bell drooled at his elbow. I heard him say, 'Blast!' and grab the receiver, whilst his snapped out, 'Yes?' would have daunted a lesser female than Aunt Meg. I knew it was her, for her voice was strong and came over in billows. 'I'm glad you liked them,' he said quietly, when some of the flow had ceased. 'They are, of course, a joint gift from my mother and myself.'

'Yes, I intend to go and see Helen,' I heard Aunt Meg reply. There was a little more back and forth, and then she rang off.

'Where was I?' he looked at me.

I lowered my eyes to my book: 'A disc protrusion was diagnosed,' I read, 'and as his drop foot persisted . . .'

'Yes, all right, I've got it now.' He carried on with the letter in a level voice, his face inscrutable.

He was polite, affable, but distant too, and he gave me no chance at all to talk to him about anything other than work, over the next two days. There are some facades you can't get behind, nor ever hope to storm. James's facade was one of those, there was nothing to catch hold of, there was nothing I could do but retreat, and hope that things would change.

Then on Wednesday evening Hugh met me out of work.

I was amazed to see him, for I knew how much he loathed hospitals. 'Good heavens,' I cried, 'surprise, surprise! How come you are here?'

'To see you, of course.'

I raised my eyebrows, and he laughed, and took my arm. 'To be honest, I'm killing time. I'm on my way to a job. I've been asked to call at Carsdale House—Robert Jenson's place. He's got some porcelain he wants to sell. I'm due there at six o'clock.'

'Now he tells me!' Carsdale House was a stone's throw from the hospital.

'So I thought,' he went on easily, 'that I'd hang about and see you.'

'You've got half an hour. We could have some tea or coffee, if you like. There's a vending machine in the hospital shop.'

'I'd rather stay here. Let's go and sit on one of those seats.' He meant in the courtyard of the old building, bounded by Casualty Block. There were gardens there, with a pool in the centre, and a rather unusual fountain shaped like a dolphin with his snout turned up to the sky. The hissing uprush of the spray and the tinkle of falling water was in my ears as Hugh and I sat down. 'I tried to get us tickets for *Heartbreak House*, he said, 'but my luck was out, they were booked solid, even the matinee.'

'Well, I'm not surprised. It's the height of the season. It's the same for any show. Aunt Meg was lucky to get her ticket, and she booked three weeks ago.'

'Yes, well, I'm disappointed. I especially wanted to see it.' He sounded like a petulant child, angry at being crossed.

'With luck you might get a cancellation.' I tried to be consoling.

He made no reply, and for several seconds we sat on the long seat, watching the dolphin spray out his water, watching nurses and doctors, and hospital workers, crossing the cobbled yard. 'Have you thought any more about what I mentioned on Saturday?' Hugh asked. He brushed some dust from his trouser leg, and his casual tone of voice gave me the clue to what he meant; he was on about Aunt Meg's will. I had hoped, so much hoped he'd not mention it again. Careful how you answer him, my warning voice cried: be plain, and firm, and definite, settle it once and for all.

'I've very sorry, Hugh,' I began, 'but I can't bring the subject up, I can't mention it to Aunt Meg. I . . . intend to leave things as they are.'

'You mean, for the time being?' I saw him start and blink.

'No, I don't. I mean for always. I can't ask her, Hugh. If *you* want to, well fair enough, but I can't ask her myself. I can't interfere with any decision I feel she made in good faith.'

'I've asked you too soon. Leave it for now, we'll talk

about it again.' He smiled at me in a stiff fashion, his face-muscles scarcely moved.

'No, Hugh. I mean what I say, and I shan't change my mind. I'm not going to raise it with her at all, not ever. It's no good trying to talk me round.'

'Are you *serious*?' His eyes narrowed.

I nodded, and mumbled yes.

'So you're hanging on to your half, are you?'

'I think that's unfair!' I flashed.

'*Unfair?*' he swerved on the seat, and gripped my upper arms, 'Unfair!' His fingers hurt, they bit through to my bones. 'You think that's unfair, do you? Well, I'll tell you what *is* . . . it's unfair, or my bad luck, that you didn't get killed in that accident! There would have been no question of halves then, it would all have been very simple! All of it . . . the lot . . . would have come to me!'

'Hugh!' I saw dislike in his eyes—patent, open dislike, perhaps even hate. I pressed myself back on the seat. He got up and walked away, stalked away from me. In a daze I saw him pass the fountain, saw him in watery outline, then clearly again as he sped through the hospital gates.

I began to shiver, I couldn't stop, my hands and feet were ice. I could hear my teeth chattering, I clenched my jaws, the shivering went on inside. I felt sick, nauseous, and the brilliant evening was ringed around with grey. I mustn't faint, I mustn't pass out, I hung like mad to the seat. And almost at once the greyness receded and I saw the fountain again, and the rainbows of water, and people approaching me.

It was two people, Ruth and James. Ruth reached me first. They must, I thought hazily, have come out of Casualty, there must be a new admission. Ruth asked me if I was all right, but I couldn't answer her, for once again that muffling greyness was coming in at the sides. A large hand forced my head between my knees.

Seconds passed, or was it minutes? I could hear Ruth's voice: 'I saw Hugh Delter flaring off. They've obviously had a row.'

'Perhaps, yes.'

'She's very upset.'

A sense of outrage hit me. They were talking about me as though I weren't there, they were talking over my head. The sheer indignity of being so treated jerked me from my torpor. I shook off James's hand, I moved and sat upright again: 'I'm perfectly all right now, but thank you for stopping,' I said. 'You're probably on your way to the ward.'

'Well, yes, we are,' began Ruth.

'Thea, if you're feeling unwell, don't attempt to drive home.' James's concern was hard to take. It nearly proved my undoing.

'I'm all right now, I'm absolutely fine,' I hurried away from them. As I did so, I heard James being bleeped, Ruth and he were still on duty. They couldn't follow, I was glad they couldn't. I made my way to the car. I let myself into its warm interior and there, in total privacy, I laid my head on the steering wheel and wept.

The new emergency admission had been a motorcycle accident case, a boy of seventeen. He was in bed three on Lytton Ward, and I saw him there next morning. He had compound fractures of tibia and fibula, and was in a split plaster. The main anxiety was his blood loss, he was on intravenous transfusion. He was febrile, and on regular four-hourly obs.

His name was Ray Norton, I made out the forms to

start off his notes. Neil came in to see him and to talk to Ruth and hand over letters for typing. Ruth was busy all morning, Ray Norton's parents arrived; they were with her some time, closeted in her room. She enquired, though, as to how I was; Ruth could be very kind. She also added a little advice, and I couldn't help wondering if she herself had followed it, so far as James was concerned. 'If you've quarrelled with Hugh, patch it up,' she said, 'don't let it drag on and on. Don't let stiff-necked pride stop you making the first move. Even if you think he's in the wrong, patch it up with him, Thea. I'm older than you, and I speak from experience.'

'It's not like that,' I told her, but of course she didn't believe me. She merely smiled and went back into her room.

As for James, he ignored it completely, much to my relief. All he said, when he came in at teatime, to give me an extra report, was: 'Perfect day for the fly past, isn't it, not a cloud to be seen. I wish I could see it, I'd like to be down on the front.'

He meant the air display, due to start at four o'clock. It was being put on by the Silver Ravens—an aerobatic team, who were flying in from further along the coast. Apparently this was an annual event, and was very popular. The Silver Ravens stunted over the sea: 'We ought to hear them coming any minute,' he said, sitting down. He began to dictate, but with a great effort, I thought.

We were half-way through a report on ankylosing spondylitis when we heard the drone of aircraft. James shot across to the window, jerked it open and leaned out, craning his neck: 'Here they are! Here they come!' I joined him at the window, he stood me in front of him:

'There now! Aren't they a glorious sight?'

I agreed that they were. His enthusiasm was infectious. He was such a . . . lovable man. Perhaps, as a small boy he had dreamed of flying a plane, dreamed of swooping and soaring over the sea. 'I suppose we'd better get on,' he said, as the silver planes dipped from sight.

'Yes,' I smiled, 'I suppose we had.' We made to move back to the desk. But we hadn't reached it, we hadn't sat down, when it happened, when it came . . . that burst of sound that split the air, that rent and clawed at it, that parted it, that rumbled it back in waves.

'God in heaven! What was that?'

'A cliff fall, it sounded like.'

We rushed to the window, which had slammed shut. James thrust it open wide: 'It's nothing like a cliff fall, nothing like . . . I think it's one of the planes!'

We exchanged glances of mutual horror. We stared out over the town. We could see nothing, the tall buildings blocked us, but way down in the street passers-by were pointing upwards, and rushing together in groups. The room behind us filled up. Ruth and two nurses were there, and several of the visitors, and a clutch of patients, all looking excited and shocked: 'What was it?' 'What's happened?' 'Was it one of the planes?' 'Where do you think it's come down?' Questions flicked around like darts, Ruth's phone began to ring, so did the one in the corridor, so did the one in the ward, so did mine: James snatched the latter up.

And after that, we all knew. He gave out the message—Casualty (our accident and emergency unit) had been put on major alert. One of the planes had gone out of control, and had crashed on the Doric Theatre. There had been an explosion, there was fallen masonry, fire had broken out. Our ward and Vinton Ward had been asked to prepare for admissions—for emergency intake. The accident team had gone out.

The theatre . . . the Doric Theatre . . . 'But my aunt's there,' I said. And I said it to the empty air, there was no one left to hear me. Ruth, in her room across the passage, was busy instructing her nurses. The visitors had gone back into the ward, so had the handful of patients. 'Aunt Meg's there,' I said again. The full awfulness of it struck home. I stood at the window and stared out in frozen apathy, watching the first ambulance leave the yard. It was followed by another, and another, and another; whilst down on the main road two fire engines hurtled by, blue lights flashing. Sirens were wailing, traffic was slowing, police cars threaded through; the whole world, or so it seemed, had been put on major alert. I could only think of Aunt Meg, only of her at that moment. And as I looked towards the west, as I looked towards the theatre, I could see a thick phalanx of smoke thrusting into the sky. It roused me as nothing else could, it jerked me into action. What I wanted to do, above all else was to rush to the scene myself, to search, and look for, to find my aunt, but I knew I couldn't do that. I wouldn't be allowed to, the area would be barred to all but the rescue teams. I had no rescue experience, I would be no use at all. But in Casualty, down in A and E, that was a different matter. I could help there, I would be of help there. I went off to find Ruth. I would tell her, yes, *tell* her I was going, I wouldn't let her stop me. I found her in the clinic room, dragging out drip-stands and cradles. Susan was with her, their backs were towards me, and I was just about to call out, when James burst through the corridor doors, he must have come from the lifts. Ruth saw him, and standing there, flattened against the wall, I heard him tell her:

'They're dividing the injured as far as possible between us, here, Wellbridge County, and the Burns Unit at Barstead. Apparently there's one hell of a mess!' He turned and looked at me. 'The first ambulance should be back any minute. They need extra help in Cas.'

'I was on my way down there,' I said shortly. Ruth didn't protest. James hustled me out and we ran down the stairs, so fast that we scarcely touched surface. I felt galvanised as though my legs were springs.

'Have you done accident work?' he asked, as we reached the ground floor at last.

'Only during my training years, but you needn't worry,' I said. 'I'm sure I can manage, I know I can help. My aunt, by the way . . .' I made my voice casual, 'was . . . *is* in the Doric Theatre.'

'Yes, I know.' He caught my glance.

'I was thinking of Uncle John.'

'He knows, he's down in Casualty now. He'll work there till a list has been got out for emergency surgery. He's very composed after his first very natural reaction of wanting to rush off to the scene. He wouldn't be any use there, he'll be vitally useful in Cas. Lady Westering may be one of the lucky ones.' James's voice held a touch of steel, but his hand through my arm, and its gentle pressure, as we hurried across the yard, belied the apparent coldness of his words.

We were crossing the courtyard, where only last evening I had sat in the hazy sunshine, watching the fountain, and hearing Hugh say it was tough luck on him that I hadn't lost my life back in the train disaster last

February. And now we had a full-scale disaster at Lowhampton. There would be loss of life and a cargo of injured. I mustn't think of Aunt Meg. If I thought of her, I couldn't help, and help was of the essence, help was needed so very urgently.

Two of the ambulances were returning already, we could hear them in the distance. I went through the doors of A and E and reported to the Doctor-in-Charge. 'Staff nurse status, manna from heaven!' He passed me over to Sister, who said much the same, and fastened a cap on my head.

Over the next two hours the stretcher-trolleys never stopped coming. It was like a conveyor-belt of trolleys, and one of the casualty nurses was detailed to stand just inside the doors and sort out the traffic. As each stretcher was wheeled in, she directed it to a free cubicle. Sometimes there wasn't a free one, and a queue of trolleys formed—a queue of waiting injured who were divided by quick assessment, into urgent, critical, or dead. There was work in plenty for everyone—a rich and tragic harvest for surgeons, doctors and ambulancemen alike.

I worked mainly with James on bone and crush-type injuries. I cut off clothing, I cleaned up wounds, I assisted with suturing. I set up drips, administered oxygen, took samples of blood for cross-matching. I comforted, and cajoled, and persuaded. My voice grew dry and husky. I lost all sense of the passage of time.

There was no news of Aunt Meg. Surely we ought to hear something. From time to time I caught sight of Uncle, working like a beaver, his face ravaged, his apron spattered with blood. It must have been agony for him, searching every trolley, looking in every cubicle for his wife.

James called me to get a drip started on a girl with a fractured hip. The ambulanceman had splinted her bad leg on to her uninjured one. She had signs of internal bleeding; she was ashen-faced and clammy; she was agitated and kept asking for her child. I had just inverted a bottle of saline over the giving-set, when Susan appeared at the cubicle entrance, making frantic signs. I said, 'Not now,' but she came right in, and behind me I heard her say:

'Lady Westering's phoned, she's got back home, just heard about the crash. She'd been out, didn't go to the matinee. I've told Sir John, of course. He's scrubbing up in Theatre Block, he said to let you know.'

'Thanks, Sue.' But what a small answer for such welcome, wonderful news. I finished the drip, I re-assured the patient, then James came in and took charge. The girl, I knew, would go straight up to theatre, and later on tonight would be comfortably settled in a bed in Vinton Ward.

Susan was still waiting outside when I left the cubicle. I wondered why, and then she told me. 'There's something more,' she said. I saw her look of consternation, she drew me on to one side. 'Thea, your aunt gave her ticket to Hugh. He was mad keen to see the show. She gave it to him only this morning. I gather he more or less asked her. He went in her place, in her stead, she's terribly upset. I suppose he hasn't . . .' her gaze swept the scene.

'No,' I said, 'he hasn't . . . at least, not so far as I know, but the injured are still coming in.' My neck went rigid, my face felt set in stone.

'I'll try to find something out,' she said, as Sister called me over. And after that I just carried on, there was nothing else I could do. I had to give mind and muscle to the job in hand, that just went on. We all stretched ourselves to the limit, we all worked as a team—one in with the other, like a smoothly ticking machine, a caring machine, composed of many skills.

The lights were snapping on in the Unit, and I was taking the paper sheets off one of the beds in the accident ward, when James called me out. 'There's some tea outside, come and get it,' I followed him out to Reception. The night staff had come on duty, they were clearing out the cubicles. Most of the casualties had been dealt with and admitted to various wards. There were still a few walking injured to be treated, they were in the waiting area. We stood on the outer rim of it, as we downed our beakers of tea. I scanned the faces, looking for Hugh's. Subconsciously, I realised, I had been looking for Hugh ever since Susan had brought down her message. Where was he . . . and what had happened to him?

'I'm worried about Hugh,' I switched my gaze from scratched, bruised faces, to the bulky form of Sister Casualty handing over her shift to a charge nurse with corrugated hair. Hugh's hair was wavy too, and dark, I bit my lip. 'I'm worried.'

James put a hand on my arm: 'I know. You must be,' he said, 'but I made enquiries. He's not been admitted here.'

'He could be at Barstead, at the Burns Hospital. Susan tried to ring Aunt Meg, but there was no reply, she's not at The Moorings.'

'And I,' James said, 'tried to get through to both

Wellbridge and Barstead Hospitals. All their lines were engaged, or they were a couple of hours ago.'

'I'll try them now, it might be easier.'

'Better for me to do it.' He took my cup. 'I'm breaking off for a little while,' he said, 'then I'm taking over from Sir John in Theatre Block.'

'And you, Nurse Westering, are to go home.' Sister Casualty came up behind us. She was still talking to me when James made his way to a nearby wall-phone. She began to recount a long, boring story about drug addicts. I scarcely heard her, I was watching James, watching him spin the dial. He was waiting, waiting for an answer. Were the lines still engaged? But no, they weren't, he had jerked to attention, his jaw was beginning to move, he was speaking, he had contacted someone—one of the hospitals. Whichever one it was gave a negative reply, for he hung up, then dialled again, then stood and waited again, rubbing the toe of his shoe against his calf. He was tired, deadly tired as I was, as all of us were. And now he was speaking, speaking again, and this time, yes, there was something. I could tell there was, for his stance altered, I saw him nod and half-turn. I could see his lips moving, his face in profile. More words, then the phone was replaced. He was coming back, he was standing in front of me.

'Is it bad? Well, tell me, tell me!' My eyes never left his face.

'He's had brain surgery, his head was injured.'

'Oh, *no!*' I stepped back a pace.

'He was taken to Wellbridge early on, he was one of the first to be rescued. He had head and face injuries, was sent into Neuro, was examined by Cecil Mallory. He got him straight into Theatre and performed a craniotomy. He suspected compression, and found it: bleeding inside the skull. He evacuated the clot and secured the ruptured vessel.'

'His chances?'

'Too early to tell. He's in excellent hands, of course. Your aunt's with him in ICU. I gather she's been there some time.'

'Oh, James, how awful!' A dozen leering spectres filled my mind. I knew the hazards of brain surgery. I dropped my head in my hands.

James's arm was round me: 'You've had enough. Come on, I'm taking your home.'

'But I ought to go and join Aunt Meg. She'll be dreadfully upset. She adores Hugh.'

'Lady Westering's all right. No arguments, Thea, please.' He stripped off my overall coat, then my cap, which got caught up in my hair grips; he jerked them out, and threw the cap down, and I all but fell against him, as he took my arm and hustled me into the yard.

'It's just the shock on top of all, on top of everything,' I said, as he levered me into the car—*his* car, the black Rover, leaving Aunt Meg's Morris on the park. How had she got to Wellbridge, I wondered? Chartered a plane, most likely, and the word 'plane' turned me sick inside again. My hands seemed to be useless, my fingers so much flab. 'Now that I'm sitting down I shall never rise again!' I tried a laugh, which ended in a sob.

'The work you did in that . . . battle area, was second to none,' he said. 'You were efficient and indefatigable, I couldn't have managed without you. So of course you're tired . . . of *course* you are. You were worried, too, about Hugh, weren't you?' I felt him glance at me.

'Aunt Meg at first, and then, yes, Hugh.' I stared out

of the window, at the winking coloured lights on the front, at the razzmatazz on the pier. Lowhampton-on-Sea was just about to start its night-time revels. Away, back in the centre of the town, lay the wreck of the theatre. Crowds would go there, to gawp and wonder. Disaster was always news, good entertainment, or at least it was to some. I shuddered. James saw me. The big car gathered speed.

'The sooner I get you home the better,' he said in staccato tones. And in my present sensitised state, his snapped-out words diminished the pleasure his earlier praise had brought.

The Moorings stood sharp and black as a cut-out, high on its shoulder of cliff. He took my key, and opened the door, came in with me, switched on lights. 'I don't like leaving you, it seems utterly wrong to do so.' I watched him tug at the cords that drooled the curtains over the windows, and I had an irrepressible urge to laugh. I wasn't amused, it wasn't amusement, more disorientation, the sudden change from there to here, from drama to normality, from noise to quiet, from crowds to James and me.

He refused a drink, but made me have one, he poured it out for me—a double brandy; the smell of it turned me sick. 'Nevertheless *drink* it,' he said. I didn't dare answer him back. It ran like cool fire down my throat.

'Now you're nursing *me*,' I choked.

'Hoist with your own petard!' He didn't sit down, he wanted to go. I knew he had to get back.

'Has Lytton Ward taken many casualties?' I was filled with brandy glow.

'Five or six. Vinton's got nine.' I saw him look at the door. Trying to make it easier for him, I got to my feet:

'It's perfectly all right. I know you must go.'

'It's a case of relieving Sir John. As soon as I do, he can get back here. And as for your aunt . . .'

'She'll stay with Hugh for as long as they'll let her. Poor Hugh!' my insides quailed. 'Whatever he said . . . what*ever*, James . . . he didn't deserve this!'

'I don't pretend to know what you mean.' He ran his hand down my cheek. 'I gather, though, that you quarrelled yesterday, and of course that makes it worse . . . for you, that is, but don't dwell on it, try not to think about it.'

'If he dies . . .'

'He may not.' He gave no false hope; he knew I couldn't be fooled. He strode across the hall, as though he couldn't wait to get out. Then he halted with his back to me, I waited and he turned. Slowly, stiffly, reluctantly almost, he held out his arms. I ran to him, ran into them, I felt them fold me close, close, so close, and his warmth was a balm, and his kiss was the comforting kind. 'Wonderful girl!' I heard his mutter, and then he was out of the door, and down the steps, and I watched him go, and I pressed my hand to my lips.

I knew I loved him . . . and I knew I always would.

CHAPTER ELEVEN

AFTER AN anxious forty-eight hours, Hugh began to recover. Aunt Meg spent most of her time at the hospital, and we had Hugh's mother with us over the first weekend. She returned to Bath on Tuesday, happy about her son. She was a much harder type than Aunt Meg. I felt she and Hugh were alike. It was five years since I'd seen her last. She told me I had grown up. But she said it with the kind of smile I didn't like very much, and she seemed to delight in mocking Mother's books. 'Alison doesn't mean half she says,' Aunt Meg remarked. But I thought she did, I thought she meant every word.

And this, my last week at St Stephen's, proved to be a busy one. With four extra patients in the ward, and one in each of the side-wards, there was little let-up in nursing or office work. I was back to forms and charts again. My burst of glory was over, until next week, when Greerton Ward at St Mildred's, London Bridge, would welcome me—I hoped—with open arms. After four months there would surely have been a complete change-over of patients. To the patients I would be a new nurse, but I would soon get to know them, of course. And as for the surgical staff I had heard (via Wendy over the telephone) that Professor Whelan was to have an assistant—a junior consultant, to whom he would hope to hand over when he retired. Wendy's ward was Genito-Urinary, so her knowledge of the ortho staff was scanty, but she told me the post had been advertised.

I wished I felt more excited about my return to Town. You don't want to go, Thea Westering, and you know the reason why. Sometimes I wished my voice-of-truth would decided to lose itself. And as for that being, the Reason Why, I only saw him in passing, passing my door to go on to the ward, passing it when he came out, passing me with a smile and a nod, always so courteous, and always accompanied . . . either by Neil or Ruth.

It wasn't until Wednesday evening, when I was crossing the main car park, that I saw him to speak to on his own. He had just finished his out-patients' clinic, his jacket was over his arm. It was a blazing evening. We were back to hot weather again: 'Hello there, how are you?' he called.

'Absolutely fine.' I had seen him coming, I had walked slowly, we halted by my car. I unzipped my bag and rootled about for my keys.

'It's good news about Delter,' he said, 'I expect you've been over to see him.'

'I haven't, as yet,' I turned to the car. 'His mother went at first; now Aunt Meg sees him every day, so I get the meals at home.'

'Oh, I see. Well, yes, I suppose Sir John's got to be fed. I mustn't detain you, must I, no doubt you're rushing home now. I've got a meeting upstairs too—no rest for the wicked, they say!' He grinned, and went off, shrugging his jacket back on.

At least he came over to speak to me, I thought, as I drove slowly home. He had made a point of stopping me, and then he seemed to retreat. He seemed as though he had something to say, then decided better of it. How many more times would I see him before I left for good? There was only tomorrow and Friday left. What was I hoping for, a miracle? I had too much sense. Miracles never happened, or hardly ever, but I prayed for one nevertheless.

I went to see Hugh next day, Thursday, Ruth gave me two hours off. Wellbridge was five miles out of Lowhampton. I got there just after four, driving through a drizzly speckle of rain. The County Hospital was larger than St Stephen's, but following Aunt Meg's instructions, I found the neuro-unit without delay. Hugh was in one of the side-wards, and Sister opened his door. 'A visitor for you, Mr Delter,' she nodded towards a chair, which I picked up and set beside the bed. I hadn't expected to feel quite so moved at the sight of Hugh lying there, heavily bandaged about the skull, his face made even more dark by a week's beard growth, to vie with his moustache.

'Scarcely a sight for sore eyes, am I?' he said, as I seated myself.

'I've seen worse.' I touched his hand. 'The main thing is how do you feel?'

'Headachy, but they help me with that, the old grey matter's all right. Everyone says I'm lucky, so I'll take their word for it. I expect something of that kind was said when you got your knee smashed up.'

'It was, yes, all the time.' I could see him looking at me. The lint-padded bandage came low on his forehead, it changed his usual expression, restricted brow movement, his eyes seemed to stay very still.

'Thea, what I said, the last time we met, I didn't mean it, you know. I shouldn't have.'

'Forget it,' I said, 'it's over and done with now. We all

say things in the heat of the moment that we don't really mean,' I smiled at him, I didn't dislike him, I would always be fond of him. I felt compassion, as well as fondness, but both of these were tempered. I wished him well, and that was the end of it.

'I very nearly snuffed it, didn't I?' he tried to shift higher in bed, and I helped him do so, plumping his pillows up.

'You gave us an anxious two days. It was a shocking time all round. Twenty-four people lost their lives, there were over two hundred injured. The dress circle crashed down into the stalls; the Doric Theatre's old. No one knows what happened yet, why the plane lost control; the pilot was killed, blown to bits, poor man.'

'I don't remember a thing, you know—not of the actual crash. The last thing I can bring to mind is Meg handing over her ticket, saying I could have it, pressing me to take it, so naturally I did. She's over-loaded with guilt now, says it was all her fault, says if she'd kept the ticket herself, I'd have been quite all right.'

'But perhaps *she* wouldn't have been!'

He ignored that, and went on: 'She's trying to make it up to me by the way of largesse.' A small smile bent his mouth, 'She's giving me her antiques—the whole lot, keeping nothing back. I must admit I'm pleased. There's a fine collection of Art Nouveau, and six Meissen figures that will make a bomb at auction, but one has to be careful, of course. I might get Elverstein's to sell them, they've got American clients. Funny how things turn out in the end, I shall do very well after all.' His eyes were closing, his lids dropping, he was very nearly asleep. I sat with him for a little while longer, I stared at his sleeping face. Then I got up and went quietly out of the room.

The hospital forecourt of tar macadam glistened black in the rain. Alongside a car exactly like James's car, I saw the beanpole figure of Hugh's surgeon, Cecil Mallory. He swung the door open and looped inside; he sat tall and thin at the wheel, rubbing the steamy window with a cloth. Without doubt Mr Mallory had saved Hugh's life—he and the ambulanceman who had picked him up.

But it was James's car that sat in the driveway of The Moorings when I got home. I eased round it. Why had he come? Uncle must have asked him. I could see them through the french windows, which were closed against the damp evening. I could hear their voices, they seemed to be arguing. I let myself in at the side door and went upstairs to change. In no way was this for James's benefit, I always changed in the evening. I put on a dress of apricot linen, knife-pleated and belted. I brushed my hair, and left it hanging loose. And as I walked back down the stairs, more slowly than I had ascended, I thought I knew why James had come; he had come to say goodbye. He was probably going to be out of the area the whole of tomorrow, for he (as well as Uncle John) did surgery over at Wellbridge. With Neil's coming more surgery fell to James.

He turned round with his customary hello as I enterd the sitting-room. Uncle was puffing by the decanter, Aunt Meg was perched on a chair. And it was no exaggeration to say that the atmosphere was electric. I could feel the tension. Aunt Meg was affected as well.

'How did you find Hugh, my darling?' she more or less pounced on me, relieved at the diversion my entrance had made.

'Incredibly well, I was very surprised,' I smiled at her anxious face.

'Thea was afraid to go, James.' And now she spun round to him. 'I think she was frightened . . . nervous of how he would be.'

'No, Aunt,' I had to correct her. 'I didn't much want to go. Being afraid didn't come into it.'

'My dear child! What a thing to say!' She looked very taken aback. She pushed a glass of sherry into my hand.

'James is leaving Lowhampton,' Uncle John said shortly. The talk about Hugh had passed him by, and as for his slapped-down statement, it left me agape, I stared wordlessly at James.

'I don't know that I am, yet. I've simply been put on a short-list. It was just that I felt,' he looked at Uncle, 'that I ought to tell you today.'

'You've put in for another job?' I edged forward a little, till I saw his face. I thought he looked rather pale.

'Yes, for a Junior Consultant's post, at St Mildred's Hospital, assistant to Professor Whelan. I'm on the short-list of six.' He sounded defensive, his jaw was set, his eye had a steely glint.

'Good gracious! *St Mildred's!*'

'It's a shock,' I heard Uncle bark.

'Wendy told me about the post. I knew it was being advertised. I hope you get it,' I was proud of my flat-sounding voice.

'He'll get it, course he'll get it, stands to reason he'll get it. The fact that he's worked with me for seven years is a credential. Added to which he's had his Fellowship for close on eighteen months. St Stephen's isn't of the size, nor type, to warrant junior consultants. Neverthe-

less, I hoped he'd stay on and take my place one day.'
Uncle John looked exceedingly down-in-the-mouth.

'You've only just turned sixty,' Aunt Meg interrupted. 'You'll most likely go on until seventy, dear, and
James must think of himself.'

Uncle continued to expostulate, I had never seen him
so rocked. 'What with James going to London, Mallory
leaving the country *and* taking Sister Filey with him, it's
the brain-drain all over again!'

'Is Ruth going to work for Mr Mallory?' The question
shot out of me. I asked it of James, but Uncle answered:
'Damn it, she's *marrying* him, gave in her notice this
afternoon. He's got a post in Switzerland! Seems like
only the other day she was going to marry you,' he glared
at James, who smiled faintly. 'I don't know what the
world's coming to. Nothing's the same for half an hour
on end!'

'But change is a fact of life, darling,' Aunt Meg tried to
calm him down. I backed to the doors and went on to the
patio.

I felt bemused, light-headed, I could hardly take in
what I'd heard. I thought about it, I struggled to think:
James might come to St Mildred's . . . to my hospital
. . . to work there . . . to work with Professor Whelan.
He would come to the ward, I would see him often, I
would be a nurse on his ward. And as for Ruth marrying
Cecil Mallory, my thoughts became more confused. Did
James mind? What did he feel? And oh, how wrong
were the gossips, for it must have been Mr Mallory's car
Miss Reenham had seen at Ruth's flat. Everything
seemed to fall into place. I remembered them at the
barbecue. Was James still in love with Ruth? Had she
jilted him for Mallory? Well, if she did she's barmy, I

thought, and I spoke the thought out loud. Behind me the talk in the sitting-room went on.

After what seemed a very long time, James came out. He sat down beside me, still looking steely-eyed. 'Things are simmering down in there. I've been asked to supper,' he said.

'Oh, good, I'm glad.'

'But I must get home, it's Angela's night off. It's too late to ask her to change it.'

'My aunt will understand.'

'She does, I've just explained to her.' He stared out at the rain. 'Can you come with me, have a meal at Northbarn? That is, if you're free. You could tell me all about St Mildred's, clue me up a bit.'

Useful Thea, I thought to myself, but I didn't intend to refuse: 'I'd love to come, thank you,' I said, 'and I'll certainly help, if I can.' I went off to tell Aunt Meg, who told me she was becoming more and more bewildered by the hour.

'Just to keep the record straight,' James said, as we drove off, 'I didn't apply for the job in London because I dislike my post here, nor because—as Sir John hinted— that I'm chasing after his niece.'

'I don't suppose he really believes either of those things, any more than I do.' I felt a little piqued. 'Uncle John doesn't want you to go; his pride is a little hurt. That's all it is. He'll come round in the end.'

'I felt I had to tell him about it, now I'm at short-list stage. But I may not get it.'

'Only time will tell that.' I stared straight ahead. I wasn't going to butter him up, and say I was sure he would. Chasing his niece . . . he'd been warning me off, and not very subtly either. Was he upset about Ruth's engagement? Had he, perhaps, nurtured hopes of her going with him, of her getting a post in Town? I didn't know. Perhaps he would tell me. Why had he asked me to Northbarn, I wondered as we turned up the short, straight drive: 'It was raining the last time I came here,' I said as I got out.

'I remember that, and it seems,' he said, 'a very long while ago. A great deal has happened since, most of it for the better. Well, come in, you're getting wet.' He drew me into the hall. Angela Tell was coming down the stairs:

'The boys are asleep, and there's plenty of casserole for two people, sir, that is if Miss Westering's staying. I'll lay another place.'

'Don't bother, I'll cope,' James said, and she smiled at us and left.

'That's what I like about Angela Tell, she's a non-fusser,' he said.

'Will she move to London with you, if you get the St Mildred's job?'

'I don't know.' His answer was short. 'I'm going to make some tea—a very large, relaxing potful, I need it, and so do you. The casserole can sit in its oven for a few more minutes. Come and sit down and make yourself comfortable.'

He showed me into a small, square room, with a big curved window that looked out over a well-trimmed lawn. There were Michaelmas daisies in the borders, and a few blown-looking roses. The lilacs were over till next year; his wife had planted the lilacs. My gaze wandered round the room, and alighted on a photo-graph, on the old-fashioned mantelshelf, just above my head. It was a school photograph of a group of children—more a play-school group. I easily picked out William and Barty, plumper and young than now. Holding their hands, with the idea, no doubt, of trying to hold them still, was a tall, thin young woman in jeans, with a wide and beautiful smile, and long hair, as straight and dark as mine. I was still looking at the photograph when James came in with the tray: 'Is that your wife?'

'Yes, that's Val, taken when the twins were three.'

'She looks . . . nice.'

'She was.'

'Do you miss her?'

He passed me my cup of tea. 'Yes, I do.' He seated himself on the other side of the fireplace. He poured out his tea, but left it on the tray. 'I miss her, but I think of her now without feeling desperate. When she first died . . . words can't describe . . . I just worked and tried to forget, to dull the sensation, for that's what it was—a pain that never let up.'

'I can understand that.' The door brushed open, Badger came in and went out. I could hear a sort of thumping shuffle, he was going up the stairs, sneaking up to join the twins, no doubt.

'I had the boys, of course,' James was reaching for his tea. He wasn't looking directly at me, and it was then that I realised he was leading up to telling me about Ruth. Perhaps he wanted to talk about her, perhaps he just wanted to talk, perhaps that was why he has asked me here tonight. 'Yes the boys helped,' he cleared his throat, 'and my mother was marvellous, but life at home was an arid, lonely place. Then I met Ruth . . .' (I felt myself tense.) 'She brought me a kind of ease. She was unhappy too, had been let down by a man she very much loved, someone she had been living with for years. She was good with the twins—a maternal type; she wanted to be married, so did I . . . I missed being one of a pair. So, we got engaged—a great mistake—two wrongs don't make a right! Almost as though that decision to marry was a catalyst (or a warning) we began to have doubts and differences of a rather important kind. Our relationship thinned away to nothing, and in the end it snapped. It was Mother's heart attack that forced the issue, in a way. Had things been right between us, *then* was the time to marry, the obvious practical time to marry, as Ruth pointed out. But we just couldn't do it . . . *both* of us took fright.'

'That . . . sounds rather sad.'

'More a lesson to be learned. At least Ruth is settled now.'

'But James, he's so much older than Ruth—Mr Mallory, I mean.'

'I think a lot of silly twaddle is talked about age, you know. Ruth and he are well suited. He can give her the children she wants, and the security, and the status. And she'll be good for him—cool, quiet, and soothing when he gets home!'

'You paint an idyllic picture.' I gave a nervous laugh. 'And, my goodness, think of all the talk, once the news gets out. You see, everyone thought that you and Ruth were still . . . were still . . .' I stopped short: 'Well, you always seemed so *friendly*!' I finished up.

'We had little to be unfriendly about, and gossip builds on nothing. Even one's own family can spark off the wrong talk at times.' He gave me one of his level looks, then drank his tea straight down. 'I suppose you and Delter intend to get married, once he's out and about. How is that going to fit in with your wish to live in Town? Would that be why you were quarrelling, that evening by the fountain?'

'Not, it wasn't, and it wasn't a quarrel. Just . . . Hugh letting off steam. And we're not getting married. I couldn't marry anyone I didn't truly love.'

'And you don't love him?'

'Not any more . . . not since years ago.'

I heard, rather than saw, James rise, and stand on the hearthrug, with his back to the fireplace, just in front of my chair. I heard him say: 'Splendid, I'm glad to hear that!' a long way above my head. I wanted to speak, I struggled to speak, but my heart was racing so hard . . . beating, beating hard in my ears, I gripped my hands in my lap. I felt as though I were poised on the edge of something so important, something so tremendous I hardly dared breath. The heathrug was pale and silky in texture, I stared at its pastel scrolls, and then I looked at James, and said in a burst of tremulous courage:

'Well, what about all those questions, the one about St Mildred's. You were going to ask me to fill you in about Professor Whelan. Don't you remember? That's why you brought me here.'

'No,' he said, 'that wasn't the reason, and I think you know it wasn't. I brought you here to ask questions, yes, but not to do with work.' He bent and drew me up out of the chair, he looked searchingly into my face. He kissed my hair, he kissed my brow, he closed my eyes with kisses. Then he moved, so that we rested together, I felt his closeness, and warmth, and his heart beating . . . racing and racing like mine. 'I brought you here to tell you I love you, and to ask how you feel about me; to ask if you have been feeling as I have, over the past four months . . . that we're made for each other, meant for each other . . . were destined, intended to meet. Those are the questions I'm asking, Thea. Do you love me at all . . . *do you love me?*' He held me from him, whilst his eyes bored into mine.

He must have read my answer there, it must have been plain to see. I didn't really need to tell him: 'Yes, oh, yes,' I said, 'you must know I do . . . you must know it . . . of *course* I love you, James! Didn't you know, surely you guessed?' The words tumbled out of me. It was such a relief to be able to say them, to speak them aloud with joy, and to see his face, and to know it was true, what I felt *he* felt too.

There was tenderness in his kiss that disarmed me, that touched the core of me, there was mounting passion that spiralled me up to the skies. How long we kissed and clung together, how long we touched and murmured, I had no idea. We lost all sense of time.

We sank down in the chair, and he drew me against his shoulder: 'I've loved you,' he said, 'since the first day we met. It was love at first sight for me. It began that afternoon I got in the train with the twins, I looked at you and I felt as though I'd been struck between the eyes.'

'But you hated me then.'

He shook his head: 'I just didn't want to love you. But I had no choice, it grew on me,' he kissed the tip of my nose, 'it grew with every passing day, it made its presence felt, it dogged my heels, it disturbed me in the night.'

'Oh, James.'

'My darling, my beautiful Thea, will you marry me? I want you in my life for always.'

'I'll marry you when you like.'

'It'll be like brand-new beginnings.'

'For all of us,' I said. I was thinking of, and including, the twins, and of course he knew I was.

'It's like a miracle,' we said together, almost as one voice.

And then we went upstairs to tell the boys.

We have been married a year now, and we live in London, five miles from St Mildred's. James got the job, and he and Professor Whelan work well together. The boys attend a day school nearby; they love their 'different' life. But at weekends, whenever we can, we motor down to Pleydon . . . to Northbarn, which we never want to sell. Angela lives there, she caretakes for us, and keeps the garden trim. She waits on us hand and foot when we go, so it's like a mini-holiday, and a rest for James, who works very hard indeed. Badger lives with us in Town, but we take him wherever we go. As the boys say, he's one of the family . . . 'and we *love* him, don't we, Thea?'

And the family will soon be increased in number, for in five months' time I hope to present my dearest James with another small son, or daughter. James would like a little girl, but although I've not told him so, what I would really and truly like is another set of twins . . . two more tawny-haired little boys.

Mills & Boon

4 Doctor Nurse Romances
FREE

Coping with the daily tragedies and ordeals of a busy hospital, and sharing the satisfaction of a difficult job well done, people find themselves unexpectedly drawn together. Mills & Boon Doctor Nurse Romances capture perfectly the excitement, the intrigue and the emotions of modern medicine, that so often lead to overwhelming and blissful love. By becoming a regular reader of Mills & Boon Doctor Nurse Romances you can enjoy EIGHT superb new titles every two months plus a whole range of special benefits: your very own personal membership card, a free newsletter packed with recipes, competitions, bargain book offers, plus big cash savings.

**AND an Introductory FREE GIFT for YOU.
Turn over the page for details.**

**Fill in and send this coupon back today
and we'll send you**

4 Introductory
Doctor Nurse Romances yours to keep
FREE

At the same time we will reserve a
subscription to Mills & Boon
Doctor Nurse Romances for you. Every
two months you will receive the latest
8 new titles, delivered direct to your door.
You don't pay extra for delivery. Postage and
packing is always completely Free.
There is no obligation or commitment –
you receive books only for
as long as you want to.